MINING FOR LOVE

MOUNTAIN MEN OF MONTANA, BOOK 2

DANA ALDEN

ISBN 979-8-9863610-1-7

AUGUST 1865, MONTANA TERRITORY

Delia couldn't believe this was happening. She'd traveled across two states and two territories to arrive in Gallatin City, Montana Territory. She'd taken a wagon to a train, to another train, to a steamship and on to a ferry across the Missouri River…to this. To a town so small, she wasn't sure it should be called a town, and certainly not a city. To the only hotel/restaurant/bar/post office in town.

To be held up at gunpoint.

She was exhausted from traveling, exhausted from trying to sleep sitting up squashed next to other smelly travelers. Exhausted from trying to sleep on a noisy, swaying boat. Exhausted from imagining what she'd find at the end of her journey…and who she'd find.

She was exhausted from guarding her few belongings. She'd brought the maximum she could manage. Everyone said it was different out here, that shopping was difficult, and to bring what was most essential.

And now, here were a couple of men waving their guns

around. No one else looked totally panicked, but no one looked relaxed and happy either. There was Mr. Daily, the proprietor. Two young men were sitting at a table near the base of the stairs, greenhorns by the look of them, another sitting very still by the window, with a worn shirt and hat that said he wasn't new to the West. And Mr. Stacey—he'd driven the wagon over from the ferry station. It was only luck that had placed him there to pick up some crates just when she arrived.

She could have walked, but not with her boxes. She'd hated the thought of leaving them there after keeping them safe all this way. It was just that so many desperate young men were milling about. They were arriving on their way to the placer mines of Alder Gulch and Last Chance Gulch. Others were leaving, finding it too hard to make a living mining, never mind making a fortune. In any case, she feared some might be so desperate as to eye her goods.

And now, again, these new desperados were poking about her stacked boxes. She was going to end up with nothing, when she'd already thought herself as close to nothing as she'd ever hoped to be.

"Whose boxes are these?" demanded the tall, skinny one with black hair and greasy beard.

Delia didn't want to answer. She didn't want to draw attention to herself. But she realized after a moment that while none of the men was pointing to her, neither did they want the personal attention of the gunmen.

"Now, Freddy," said Mr. Daily, leaving his hands on the bar top carefully, but speaking confidently. "You know I have an agreement with Ned Bart. You shouldn't be in here bothering me or my patrons."

Delia saw that his speaking distracted the two trouble-makers and allowed Mr. Stevens to unholster his own weapon. The man sitting near the window held very still but, she thought, poised for action.

Freddy said, "We're not bothering you." He moved his gun down, holding it alongside; he pointed it at the floor, but didn't holster it. His friend kept his gun high and swung around to aim at Mr. Stevens, who stilled perfectly. "We're here to greet the young lady."

He turned to Delia and she felt herself freeze. Was this more than a robbery? Oh, Lord, she thought, please help me.

"Freddy, you leave her be." Mr. Daily suddenly had his own gun in hand, resting on the bar top, cocked and aimed toward Freddy.

"Don't get your knickers in a twist, Daily," said Freddy with a sly smile, his eyes on Delia as he walked. "I just want to chat."

He'd reached Delia's table by then. He pulled out a chair and sat down, half facing her and half facing the rest of the room. He had rotten, yellow teeth and disgusting breath that made Delia lean back when he spoke to her.

"What's your name, little miss?"

Delia looked over at Mr. Daily, hoping for a clue as how to proceed. He gave her a slight nod.

"Mrs. Cordelia Watson."

She saw a flicker of…something…in his eyes.

"You married?"

"Yes. No. Uh, widowed." She could tell by how he nodded in response that he somehow thought that was better than being married.

"What brings you to our neighborhood?" he asked as he tipped his chair back onto two legs. He proceeded to rock it back and forth.

She wasn't sure what to say. She wanted him to think she had support, that she wasn't a lone woman in the middle of nowhere with no protection. But she didn't want to lie, to get him angry if he found out.

"Family."

He sat forward eagerly. "Family. A brother?"

"No," she answered too quickly, because she could tell that was the answer he wanted.

"No," he paused, and then gave that sly smile again. "Are you here to visit your mother?"

His friend across the room laughed. Delia knew there were so few women out here that he'd never believe it, even if she thought she could bluff her way through the interview. She glanced around the room and caught the eye of the man by the window. She realized everyone in the room was listening intently.

"My fiancé."

Freddy leaned forward so quickly his chair legs slammed into the floor with a bang. Delia flinched. He asked, "Do you mean Samuel Emerson?"

She could tell her answer was important and was so relieved she could say truthfully, "I don't know that gentleman. My fiancé is Mr. Calvin Ayers."

Freddy and his friend both looked surprised. "Mountain Man Cal?"

"I don't know him by that name."

Freddy looked at her speculatively, trying to decide whether to believe her.

"I have a letter." She reached for her carpetbag and then froze when she saw Freddy had pulled out his gun. It was aimed directly at her.

CHAPTER 2

From his seat by the window, J.B. Wood could see that Mrs. Cordelia Watson was terrified. He had hoped these two men would get the information they were seeking and get out, but now he wondered if he'd misjudged. He didn't like the way Freddie was waving around his gun, which looked like a Colt Pocket Navy Revolver, probably left over from the war.

J.B. slowly moved his hand toward his own gun. The 5-shot Kerr's Patent Revolver was engraved with a scene of a stagecoach holdup and J.B. couldn't help but think it was appropriate to the drama unfolding in front of him.

"In my bag, I have a letter…" the pretty woman said with a shaky voice. After a moment, Freddy nodded. The woman continued to reach in her bag and pulled out a book. Tucked in its pages was a letter. She held it out with a shaking hand. Freddy took it from her, allowing his fingers to touch hers. She shuddered and a look of revulsion crossed her face.

Freddy studied the letter briefly and then tossed it back to her. He stood up so quickly she gasped.

"You ain't the lady we're looking for."

Freddy holstered his gun. J.B. let his fingers begin to slide away from his own weapon, until Freddy leaned his lanky form over Mrs. Watson, reaching out to finger the collar of her dress.

"Oh!" she exclaimed and slapped his hand away. Her eyes turned to saucers when she realized how her instinctual reaction might be taken by the dangerous Freddy. It felt like everyone in the room stopped breathing. But he only laughed, and said, "I'll see you around, Missus Watson," emphasizing the Mrs. as though to point out that she didn't have a Mister to stand between them.

Then Freddy turned and nodded to Mr. Daily. Ignoring everyone else, he gave a *let's go* tilt of his head to his partner, and they sauntered out the front door.

J.B. Wood tilted his chair back to look out the window. He wanted to be sure those two rats were good and gone. He watched them untie their horses and head out toward the south. Ned Bart was supposed to have a base somewhere between Bozeman and Virginia City. It was largely so unsettled outside the explosively growing mining towns, that the nasty gang could be well hidden almost anywhere.

Once J.B. was sure they weren't coming back, he settled his chair back down. Daily and Stevens were uncocking their guns and wiping sweat from their brows. There were two young men sitting at a round table. One looked green with stress while the other looked thrilled with the action, or near action, he'd just seen. J.B. thought this naïve newcomer wouldn't be so smiley if there had been actual shooting. Nothing romantic about a man's innards torn open and a painful death. He's seen too much of that in the War.

Sometimes, he tired of all the newcomers moving to the territory, but he wouldn't mind a little more civilization. And if that included some beautiful women like the one sitting across the room from him, all the better. He wondered if he should go talk to her. Her hand was still shaking as she brought a cup of

Dutch courage to her lips. Daily was encouraging her to drink the libation he'd just brought over.

He also wondered if Cal knew he had a fiancée. He'd just seen his friend and mining partner the previous month and Cal had said nothing about getting married. Had this gal just known Cal's name and made up a story to sidestep the two gunmen? But she'd had a letter. J.B. wasn't sure how well Freddy could read, but enough, he suspected, to read a simple letter.

The woman, Mrs. Cordelia Watson, was staring into her cup, gripped between her two hands resting on the tabletop. She had lovely brown hair pulled back in a braided bun at the base of her neck. She had pale skin with some pink on her cheeks and forehead, showing the effects of the strong western sun. She was slender but sturdy-looking, a well-off daughter of a farmer, or even a grocer in town. She had dark circles under her eyes, emphasized by the paleness her shocking experience had brought on.

She had to be tough, J.B. thought, to have traveled here on her own—because she clearly *was* alone—and to have been inquisited by Freddy at near gunpoint and not have collapsed in vapors.

And, he thought, *maybe I ought to stop admiring her so much, if she's indeed going to be Cal's bride.* With that, he made the decision to introduce himself and see how he could aid her.

He stood up, walked over to her, and sat down beside her. He knew his mama back home would think his manners poor for not introducing himself first, but he didn't think she was ready for niceties, now he could see how white-knuckled her grip on the cup was. Nor did he want to have his back to the door for long, in case any more troublemakers showed up. Word of a beautiful young woman, unprotected, would travel fast.

"Pardon me, Mrs. Watson. I couldn't help overhearing you

and Freddy just now." He didn't continue because her eyes looked so upset, he thought she might run screaming. Maybe not as tough as he'd first surmised. "Are you alright, Ma'am? Those ruffians are gone now."

"Yes, thank you." Her voice was low and strained. She watched him warily and he realized she wasn't to know he meant her no harm nor importuning.

"I'm J.B. Wood, of Virginia City. I'm a business partner, and friend, of Cal's."

She looked surprised at that, but it seemed to distract her from her anxiety. Her big green eyes searched his face. She was even prettier up close than she'd seemed from across the room, though now he could see the coating of travel dust covering her from head to toe.

"I was hoping to find Calvin here, in this...town." She looked around the room, as though looking around a whole town, and she nearly was. "He has his mail delivered here." She seemed bewildered, her eyes getting glassy.

He felt the corners of his mouth tilt up slightly. What counted for a town in the territories wasn't the same as back east. He remembered having to grow accustomed to the differences. She was just starting out. "He does have his mail delivered here, but he only comes in once a month or so." Her focus sharpened momentarily, her eyes meeting his again.

"Do you know when he's due? Or perhaps I can hire a ride to his...home?"

She didn't seem to know much about his friend, and again J.B. wondered whether Cal knew he had a fiancée anywhere, never mind here, waiting for him. What he did know, watching her sway slightly, was that she was beyond exhausted.

"I think you're best off waiting for Cal here, if he hasn't directed you elsewhere." She sagged a little. "Have you arranged a room with Daily here?"

She shook her head. "I've only just arrived."

"I'll set it up." As he stood up to walk to the bar, he felt her unease at taking help from a strange man, while still being overwhelmed enough to need that help.

He spoke quietly to the hotelier, "Have you got a room for her?" At the nod, he added "And a room next to it for me?" He handed over some coin, received two keys, and walked back to Mrs. Watson. She was already lost in her cup again, with vacant, glazed eyes.

"Let me take you to your room." The poor thing, so exhausted, glanced from him, to the stairs, to her boxes, confused and wary. "I'll carry your boxes to your room. You can lock yourself in. I'll sleep in the room next door and listen for any trouble."

Mrs. Watson's eyes teared up. The green eyes became a brighter green. Maybe Cal knew what he was up to. In any case, J.B. would look out for his friend's fiancée and keep her from harm.

Mrs. Watson stood and J.B. aimed her toward the stairs before stooping to pick up her boxes. There were three. One big one with a rope handle that he tossed onto his shoulder. The other two, he balanced on his hip under his arm. He followed her up the stairs.

As her skirts disappeared down the hall, he suddenly turned to find every single man in the bar gazing wistfully where Mrs. Watson had just been. He paused, turned toward them fully, and one by one met each and every man's eyes. He was fairly sure they understood his message. *Back off.*

CHAPTER 3

Delia woke up to find the dust motes dancing in the strong sunlight pouring through the thin white cotton window curtain. She felt, at last, like a person again. She was hungry and could tell she had slept through the night and into the next day. She also remembered the men with guns, and the man who had helped her to this room. It seemed he knew Calvin. Hopefully, this Mr. J.B. Wood could help her find him.

She used every drop of water in the pitcher to scrub herself clean. She brushed and rebraided her hair, then shook out her last clean dress to wear. She had let the other ones get so dirty, dusty and sweaty in travel, but couldn't hold out anymore. It didn't look like there was a laundress in this little place, but perhaps she could do her own washing? She'd probably have to take in laundry to pay for her room if Calvin didn't show up soon. She tried to smile at her own joke, but it was too close to the truth to be funny.

Delia closed and locked the door behind her, then walked softly to the stairs. She wanted a moment to peek over the banister and make sure that Freddy fellow hadn't returned. She saw Mr. Daily behind the bar again, those two young men sitting at the same table as the day before, two more strangers, and Mr. Wood. He was, she realized, quite handsome. Yesterday, she had been too tired to notice anything except that her wariness of him was not enough to set off alarm bells, and at the time, that was all she could do to assess him.

Mr. J.B. Wood had brown hair with red highlights. His skin was weathered and swarthy, like that of all the men she'd seen, except some of the newcomers. He had broad shoulders and a slender waist. He had carried her boxes, she remembered, but she hadn't noticed if he'd struggled or not.

He certainly looked strong. He was standing at the bar with the other men she didn't recognize, all listening to the bartender read from a newspaper. She guessed it had come in the mail pouch on the same ferry on which she had traveled.

She looked back to Mr. Wood to see him looking back at her. He gave an imaginary tip of the hat to her, though his hat was actually resting on the bar in front of him. Her dealings with him were limited, and though his manners weren't by the book, his actions all spoke of respect. It was interesting, to say the least, how many men she'd met during her travels who demonstrated good manners, but the demeanor behind them had negated their behavior. And then there were some whose manners weren't so nice, but a good-humored and sincere personality had made all the difference for a few of them.

Delia started. She had been woolgathering. For the last few weeks, she'd been on her own. She had already gotten used to not having anyone waiting on her. She headed down the stairs, and despite having to give attention to ensure her dress didn't catch on the rough wood of the treads, she knew every eye was upon her. Her dress was sky blue with little yellow flowers flecked across it. It was an older dress, but neat and clean and made her look pretty, as her mother had said whenever Delia wore it.

Mr. Wood met her at the bottom of the stair. "Good afternoon, Miss Delia."

"Good afternoon, Mr. Wood."

"Come sit at this table, if you will. I'm sure you are hungry. Daily saved a lunch plate for you."

Her stomach rumbled and she felt her cheeks blush lightly. "Oh, yes, thank you. And thank you for your assistance yesterday. I was so very exhausted from the travel."

He looked at her seriously. "And probably by your welcome committee. Do you have any connection to this Samuel Emerson he asked about?"

"No. I am not acquainted with him – or even his name."

He gave a satisfied nod. "Good. He's in some trouble with some bad characters." She had a feeling she'd be in real trouble right now if she had answered wrongly yesterday. They walked a few steps to the same round table she'd sat at the day before. J.B. seated her and then chose a chair, adjusting it to give himself an unimpeded view of the door out onto the porch.

Delia was wondering how worried she should be that more ruffians might walk in that door when her thoughts were interrupted.

"So, does Cal know to meet you?" Mr. Wood asked.

This question startled Delia. While it was possible a letter had gotten lost, it wasn't something she had considered. Of all her worries and anxieties, not being met at the end of her journey had not been one of them. What if Calvin didn't know to meet her? How long would it take to find him?

"So, he doesn't know?"

"I don't know. Letters were sent, but I left before he could have responded to the one with the plan. I thought he knew, but now I can't be sure." She felt foolish in front of this handsome man for not being able to say, "Of course he knows!" Shouldn't one's fiancé be dependable? Shouldn't they be close enough, even through letters, to know such important information as where in the world one's soon-to-be husband or wife was?

And yet, Delia knew she had to leave Missouri when she did, that waiting for a final letter had not been an option.

"It's just that," Mr. Wood lowered his voice and glanced around, "Cal has never mentioned you to me. It seems like something he would do."

Delia realized he was skeptical of her engagement, her claim to connection. Part of her wanted to prove herself to this man, for the sake of pride and continued aid—and because, to be honest, she didn't like the idea of him thinking poorly of her. The other part of her was angry that a near stranger thought to doubt her, and that rather than walk away in a huff, she had to try to assure him enough to keep helping her. While she would find a way to figure things out, having a local guide —and protector— would help.

She didn't really know how Calvin felt about this, either. That was, his father had assured her Cal was looking forward to a wife and remembered her fondly, but she realized now that was not the same as looking forward to *her* as a wife. Could she have fooled herself so thoroughly? Or was it simply that Mr. Wood's questions reflected his lack of knowledge of the situation, and not hers?

Delia was given a further moment to think by the arrival of her plate. Mr. Daily brought her a thick slice of ham with mashed potatoes and boiled carrots. He lay the plate in front of her, and then from his back pocket he pulled a napkin rolled around a knife and fork. With a quick nod, he headed back behind his bar.

"Calvin and I grew up together." Mr. Wood's eyebrows rose with a question in them, so Delia elaborated. "In Missouri. Our farm adjoined both his grandfather's farm and his father's farm."

That did it, she saw. To know his home state, and that he grew up next door to his grandfather, would be sufficient. And thank goodness. She was here to start over. Having to recount all that led to this big change would not help her fit in here. She took her knife and fork and began to cut her ham. Having satisfied the basic curiosity of Mr. Wood, she was free to give in to her hunger. And boy, was she hungry!

I t was late. Or, it was early, depending on how you looked at it. But in either case, J.B. had no trouble seeing the trail in front of him. It was lit by the light of a million stars. The flat land around him, open prairie covered with the dark outlines of sagebrush, melted away under the glowing dome of the pinpricked sky above him. He could see the mountains in the distance only by the absence of light, the lack of stars. Even after living out West for more than a year, he was still awed by the majestic beauty of the landscape. Even when he didn't want to be seeing it.

He hadn't expected to be out till all hours of the night. He'd left the hotel that afternoon, after seeing that Mrs. Watson was safe for the time being, in order to go hunting. Where he lived, in Virginia City, the local game was being depleted by the huge influx of miners. What wasn't already killed was scared away by the hubbub of thousands of men packed along one little creek.

He'd successfully bagged a pair of prairie grouse. His mouth watered, thinking of how fresh-roasted grouse would taste. He was on his way back when he'd spotted some Indians passing in the distance and had hunkered down rather than risk meeting a group who might or might not have been friendly.

So here he was, dragging into Gallatin City terribly late, or quite a bit early. The town was quiet. Most of the folks who'd come in on the ferry the day before had already headed out for one mining town or another. Some headed north to Last Chance Gulch. Some headed south to Virginia City, Central City, and other pop-up mining towns in Alder Gulch. He'd heard some men were looking for gold in the Big Belt Mountains to the north, too.

J.B. had a couple of friends keeping an eye on his claim, looking out for unwanted visitors, but even so, he really hated to leave it for long. Only because he needed to give Cal the important news, news that he wouldn't write down in a letter, was he here.

And now his thoughts returned to the second reason he had to stay. He couldn't leave Cal's fiancée here all alone. If J.B. had a woman, he'd expect his friend to look out for her, and surely Cal could expect the same of him. He could post a letter to Cal in Bozeman, or ride out there himself, but he couldn't be sure Cal would be there. He guessed he ought to discuss this all with Mrs. Watson tomorrow. But in any case, as soon as he figured out what to do with Mrs. Watson, he would hotfoot it back to Virginia City.

Meanwhile, he would catch a couple of hours of sleep in his hotel room before tracking her down.

J.B. AWOKE WELL INTO THE MORNING. HE DRESSED AND HEADED downstairs. There was no one around except Mr. Daily, standing behind the bar. J.B. walked over and handed over his room key for Mr. Daily to store in the cubby mounted on the wall.

"Hold on, Mr. Wood." Daily held out a letter to J.B. "Your friend Cal Ayers left a letter to post to you. I guess I can just hand it over."

J.B. froze in the middle of reaching for the paper. "Cal? He's here?"

"He was," said Mr. Daily, nodding. "But he headed back to Bozeman at dawn."

J.B. wanted to kick himself. Cal had been here, and he'd missed him. He took the letter to the bench on the porch outside, where there was more light.

He read what Cal wrote with disbelief. *I've been packing over the Bridger Mountains with this gal Amanda. Ned Bart's got it in for her brother and her. I told one of his boys that she's my fiancée so they wouldn't know who she really is. I can't have Delia around here telling folks she's my fiancée or Bart will figure out that Amanda's the one he's looking for.*

Poor Mrs. Watson. She was at the end of her rope and just hoping and praying Cal would show up soon to bail her out. She'd traveled all this way thinking Cal would marry her, and even if this were a temporary setback, she'd surely be hurt by the situation. J.B. also wondered why his friend had never mentioned his fiancée. But, then, it was months since they'd seen each other.

J.B., I need your help. Take Delia to V.C. and help her get settled. I'll be along as soon as I can get things settled here. But you should know, I'm hoping I can get Amanda to marry me when this ordeal is over.

J.B. read this paragraph three times. *Take her to Virginia City?* He had a mine to dig. Dammit, it was about to pay off; he just knew it. He had been hoping to find Cal and get him to come help. They could take turns digging and sleeping, and the claim would never be left unattended. Once folk heard about a strike, it wasn't safe to leave it be. And Cal wanted him to nursemaid his ex-fiancée?

P.S. Delia has a box of supplies that I ordered for you: New scales, quicksilver, and an ingot mold.

J.B. let the note fall to the ground. He sat forward on the bench, his elbows on his knees and his head in his hands. He'd never received a package with such a high delivery fee.

CHAPTER 5

Delia was in shock again. She sat in a corner of the hotel parlor, nursing her sassafras drink, wondering what to do. She'd come all this way, mentally and physically shedding her old life and preparing for her new one, and it was a bust. She was stranded in a town with barely eight buildings – and that included the barns – with enough money to last her perhaps two weeks. Not enough to go back home, if she even wanted that. Which she didn't.

She wanted to start over, afresh, in a new place, with a new husband. And that was the problem, because her fiancé didn't want her.

She and Calvin hadn't seen each other or even written since he left Missouri ten years before, but they'd been true childhood friends. It was his father who had suggested that she'd never be able to move on from the death of her husband Stephen if she stayed in town near Stephen's relatives. Mr. Ayers had acknowledged that Calvin wasn't likely to ever move back to Missouri, but the father still wanted his son to settle down with a family. So, he had suggested the engagement and written directly to Cal.

Calvin had said they had to see each other again, to see if they suited after all these years. She had agreed. *She had agreed.*

Delia wanted to kick herself. She had thought it was a mere formality, to make sure they weren't, at the very least, repulsed by each other. But she was a good-looking woman with plenty of housekeeping skills. She and Cal had been friends. It had never occurred to her that he might reject her.

She'd been sitting on a bench in the shade of the porch yesterday afternoon, admiring the vast openness, and the mountains in the distance. A hawk glided in lazy circles above. Everything was gold in the late summer heat, except right along the river where it greened up. This handsome man, with traces of the boy she had known, showed up and for a moment she had relaxed, thinking her journey was over. But then he'd started talking about this other gal…

In her heart, she knew that Cal had gone and met another woman he actually wanted to be with. He wasn't so much rejecting Delia as choosing someone else. But it still hurt her pride. And, still left her in a precarious situation.

Perhaps even harder to handle was that after all this, he wasn't even sticking around to help her out. His new woman friend was in trouble, worse than Delia's trouble, and he had to help her, the other her, first. So, he'd headed off first thing this morning, and Delia hadn't even had time…well, hadn't made time, to tell him the full extent of her troubles.

She must have been lost in thought because she was startled by the scrape of a chair. J.B. Wood sat down beside her. He looked inquiringly at her face, and she could tell he knew what was going on, yet didn't know what kind of response to expect from her. Delia wasn't even sure how she would deal with all of this. *Cry. Scream. Soldier on.*

Then, J.B. spoke and shocked her. "You know, there's a lot of fellows that will be glad to find out you're on the market." He said it with a kind smile and she knew he meant to make her feel better. But, instead, the bottom dropped out of her stomach. She couldn't marry another man. She didn't want to have to even discuss it or come up with explanations that could be argued against. It was instinctual and instant, but the words that came out of her mouth surprised her as much as Mr. Wood.

"I'm not giving up on Calvin. He's just trying to help out this poor woman. He'll be back."

J.B. sat back in his chair. He opened his mouth, but no words came out. He closed it. He didn't say a word, for which Delia was grateful.

"And I'm fine with that. It's the Christian way; to help others in need." Delia spoke rapidly, scared of the truth. "But I'm going to need to figure out what to do until then. Cal said he would ask you to help me."

J.B. slowly nodded. He put his calloused hand over hers on the tabletop. "Mrs. Watson," he said in a low, calm voice, "Cal left a note. He seems mighty taken by this Amanda gal. He might not be coming back, in the way that you mean, that is."

Delia's courage faltered. As much as she wanted to be honest with Mr. Wood, she needed to be considered 'off the table.' She just couldn't have anyone think she was available for courting. She didn't want J.B. to think badly of her -- and right now, he seemed to think she had fallen off her rocker – but, *well, it can't be helped,* she told herself.

"I don't think so," she said emphatically, pulling her hand out from under his and straightening her shoulders. "I spoke with him last evening. He'll be along and we'll get married. Meanwhile—"

She lifted her eyebrows at Mr. Wood and waited. J.B. studied her, like she was a wild animal that he wasn't sure how to approach. He even glanced around as though looking for help. Finally, he gave her a strained smile.

"Meanwhile, Cal asked me to look out for you until he was out of trouble and able to help his old friend. I will."

Delia looked at this big scruffy man with too-long hair, sun-weathered creases around his eyes, and, whew, odiferous clothes. He had beautiful, soulful brown eyes aimed at her, offering her help, aid… caring. Genuine, sincere, looking-out-for-a-fellow-human-being sort of caring. He knew what she said about Cal was foolish, but was willing to let her cling to her hope. Or at least, what he thought was her hope.

It was silly after all that she'd been through, but this was what was going to make her cry. She looked over his shoulder and focused on the glass liquor bottle, half-filled with a brown liquid, sitting on the shelf behind the bar. She stared hard but could feel the tears welling in her eyes.

"Let's take a walk." J.B. grabbed her arm and hauled her to her feet. She guessed he didn't want to see her crying all over him and thought a walk would distract her. "Let's go to the river."

They left the hotel and followed a small path through a prairie meadow, ushering her around ground cactus and sagebrush. The sun was harsh; she wished she were wearing her bonnet. It would block the light. It would hide her eyes.

They walked close, with J.B. offering his arm on the uneven spots, but didn't speak. She kept taking deep breaths, trying to calm the welling tears away. When they finally reached the shade of the tall cottonwood trees along the riverbank, he stopped and turned her to face him, with one hand on each of her upper arms.

"It's private here. A good place to cry. Do you want company or should I take a walk?" He pointed with his thumb where the path continued along the riverbank.

Delia couldn't even answer him. She didn't even know what she wanted. The tears spilled out of her eyes and she felt her face screw up, an ugly face for an ugly sob. She looked at the buttons on his shirt as best she could through the tears. What could she say? She didn't want to be alone, but she didn't want to be seen crying these loud, noisy sobs.

J.B. took the decision from her. He led her to a downed log. He sat down and pulled her down beside him on the gnarly cottonwood bark. He laid his arm across her shoulders, his hand cupping her shoulder. He gave her a comforting squeeze and looked off down the river. She leaned into him, into this near stranger, and cried her heart out. It was exhaustion. It was a dead husband, a journey, a failed fiancé. It was fear and humiliation and everything bad she'd felt and experienced in the past six months.

After she finished crying, after the sobs turned to gasping breaths, then after those turned to sniffles, after she finally ran out of tears and breathed normally again, she pulled away, but only slightly. She didn't want to dislodge his arm from around her. They both looked out onto the river, where a splash showed a fish rising to catch a grasshopper that had hopped too far. He turned his head and looked at her face. She knew she was over the worst of it when she was concerned with how red and puffy her eyes looked to him.

"Do you have sisters?" she asked.

He smiled, "Two. How'd you guess?"

Calvin had told her she could trust J.B. She analyzed his face, his recent actions and words. She'd learned that all had to match if you wanted to trust someone.

"Just a wild guess."

J.B. took his arm from around her and stood, offering that same arm again to help her rise. "Let's walk and talk. We've got to figure out a plan for you."

Delia felt a welling of gratitude, until J.B. spoiled it by adding, "Cal asked me to help you so I guess I'm obligated."

They meandered down the trail. J.B. would periodically reach down to pick up a stone. Sometimes he showed her the rock, pointing out colors or variations he found interesting. Some of them he pocketed. Some he skipped across the river.

Once, he paused to point to a faint track, long and skinny, in the dust. She followed his pointing finger until she saw the snake curled in the shade of rock. It was shades of brown with a black tongue flicking out. They continued on.

"You know a lot about rocks."

"I am a miner, you know. It helps to know rocks and sand and whatnot. This pretty green one is just a mud stone, but it's fine for skipping." He threw it across the river's surface where it bounced five times before sinking. "Sometimes, I go up in the mountains to look at the different kinds of rocks I can find up there. There's no one else around. I feel like I'm closer to God." J.B. squatted down, poking at a translucent rock, his eyes trained at the ground. "Quartz," he mumbled.

"Do they call you Mountain Man? Like that man called Calvin *Mountain Man Cal*?"

"What? Oh, no," he said, rising back up to look Delia in the face. "That's left over from Cal's trapper days. I was never a trapper. I feel like a mountain man, though. I can't imagine living anywhere else." His gaze turned to the far-off mountains you could see in every direction. He looked lost in thought, but then turned his eyes back on her and his words showed he would not be distracted.

"Are you sure you don't want me to help you find someone else to marry? In case it doesn't work out with Cal? You might even find a fellow you like better."

"What? No!" She was perhaps too emphatic, from the look on his face, but she meant it. Coming out here to marry Calvin had seemed a way to start over, but now, scary as it was, she was free to truly start again. *No one here knows me*, Delia thought, *and I can forget the past. I won't have to explain anything.*

"I've been married and wouldn't repeat it with most men."

J.B. raised his eyebrows.

She quickly added, "Except with Cal. I'll marry Cal." Then she looked down to carefully and far too slowly pull her skirt loose from a sagebrush branch that had hooked the fabric. When she finally looked up, J.B.'s eyebrows had returned to their regular position. J.B. and Delia continued to stroll until J.B. spoke. "Maybe you want to go home, back to your parents I mean, until Cal gets things worked out here?"

She shook her head. "They passed two years ago; scarlet fever." Before J.B. could respond to that, she said, "I think I need a job."

She was, she realized, free. No husband. No parents. If she could make a living, and everyone said that anyone willing to work hard, even women, could make a living out here, then she could remain free. She could be her own woman.

"Could you help me figure this out, Mr. Wood?" She needed to know if he'd really help her, that he wasn't simply paying lip service to her.

J.B. didn't hesitate. "I'd be honored, Mrs. Watson."

And then he fell over.

CHAPTER 6

Delia had been looking at him like he was a knight in shining armor, and then he tripped and fell. J.B. could feel his face burning red. He brushed the dusty dirt from his shirtfront and then prepared to rise. Instead, Delia exclaimed, "Oh my goodness!" and knocked him back down. "Don't move! Don't move!"

While she pushed on his leg and shoulder, he squirmed around trying to sight a gun, or a bear, or something that would cause her to act so. He didn't hear anything, even a rattle.

"Don't move. I'll go get help! Someone to carry you!" Her eyes were darting around, looking for someone to flag down.

"Mrs. Watson, I am fine. I just tripped." He put his hand underneath himself to push up and flinched when he felt a cactus spur embedded in his palm.

"No, no, Mr. Wood, you must be in shock. You are not fine." She studied his face, but it was hers that looked pained. It wasn't until she turned to look at his foot that he saw what concerned her. His boot was creased right across the middle, turning up so the end of his foot would have to be broken to point up and backward toward his knee.

Normally, he'd have continued to be embarrassed for falling, but now he just had to laugh at the two of them on the ground. Most people noticed his limp, but on their walk, she'd been so distraught she surely missed it.

He reached out and took each of her hands that were threatening to worry him into the ground. He held them together between his, and looked her in the eyes. Slowly and calmly, he said, "Thank you, but I am not injured nor am I in shock. That is just my boot."

She looked confused, and he didn't blame her. He set her hands into her lap and reached down to pull off his boot. Instead of a normal foot, there was the sock-covered stub. His foot had been amputated about an inch before where his toes would be. She couldn't see it because of his sock, but the knobby end of his leg was a mess of scar tissue.

"Oh," was all she said, staring at his shortened foot.

"Battle of Wilson's Creek in Missouri. Canister shot from a 3-inch rifled cannon bolt, courtesy of the Yanks from the Phoenix Iron Company in Phoenixville, Pennsylvania. Some hot metal cut off and cauterized a lot of it and the doctors did the rest."

He watched her carefully. Some folks, especially women, were squeamish when it came to these types of injuries. Instead, she looked at him in awe.

"You didn't turn septic? You're walking like normal? How is that possible?"

He smiled. He had been amazed it didn't turn gangrenous, then further amazed when it healed enough to try walking. He was glad she was as impressed as he was.

"Somehow, it healed up without infection, thank the good Lord. I was sent home and my sisters helped care for me. And then I figured out how to wrap it. I used a cane for a long time."

"Well, I'll be. You are truly a clever man."

He felt his blush returning. "I don't know about that. I persevere, that's all."

And then he found himself saying things he normally kept locked up inside. "I just couldn't stand the thought of never walking again. I know I could use crutches or a cane, but didn't want to be dependent. I didn't want folks to dismiss me, as they do, as a war cripple. That's part of the reason I came out here. I don't have to walk far as a miner, can ride my horse for longer distances, and most folks don't think anything about a limp. For the nosiest, I simply say, Battle of Wilson's Creek, and that suffices."

Mrs. Watson nodded. "I didn't even notice your limp, Mr. Wood."

"That's because you were distracted."

Now it was her turn to blush. They both laughed. He took a moment to adjust his sock and slide the boot onto his foot. That boot was starting to fold up on him more often; he'd have to figure out a solution or he'd be on the ground a lot.

He stood up and offered his hand to Mrs. Watson, even though she was already half risen. She put her hand in his anyway and he tucked it into the crook of his arm as they started to walk back along the path.

"Call me J.B. That's what my friends call me. You should, too."

She looked down for a moment, and then smiled her sweet smile. "And you shall call me Delia."

They didn't speak on their way back to the hotel. J.B. realized that though he didn't really want to be responsible for Mrs. Watson—for Delia—there were worse people to be forced into company with.

CHAPTER 7

Delia turned so her back was to J.B. She bent over and lifted her skirt so that she could unhook her stockings and slide them off. She glanced back. J.B. was carefully tying up the horses, taking far more time than he likely needed to. She placed her folded stockings on top of her shoes and then turned to the reason they had stopped in this location for a break.

It was a natural hot spring, roughly dug out to create a small pool. Logs laid along the side gave a place to sit or enter the water without getting muddy. Delia chose a spot with her back to the sun and slid her feet into the water, arranging her skirts to cover her knees without dropping into the pool.

She closed her eyes. It was heavenly.

She heard a small splash and opened her eyes to see J.B. sitting down beside her, sliding his feet and calves into the water. He had rolled up his pants to his knees. He leaned forward, sliding his hands into the warm pool. She wondered if they ached.

"Who built this?" Delia asked.

"Of course, the spring has always been here as far as

anyone knows, but sometime in the past year, some miners dug it out and laid the logs around it. Mining is back-breaking work." J.B. wiggled his fingers in the water. "Hand-breaking work, too."

They sat in peaceful silence for a while, until J.B. asked, "What's that smell? Is it you?"

Delia sputtered. She had noticed the smell, too, but thought it came from the water. "What? No! That's not me. It's the water. Or the...the—" She looked around for some plant or animal that could be causing the smell.

J.B. started laughing. Delia was confused, and then annoyed. J.B. leaned back on his hands and smiled. "Oh, Delia! That was funny!"

"I don't think so," she said, and even to herself she sounded stuffy. She tried to smile and pretend she hadn't been mortified to be accused of smelling so terribly.

"Yes, it's the water. Sulphur. Some say the rotten egg smell is how you know it's good healing water."

They returned to silence. Delia looked at the canyon walls surrounding them, wondering what critters could be hiding up among the bushes and scrub trees, watching them.

After a bit, they got back on J.B.'s horse, the one he had hired out of Virginia City. Delia was riding up behind him on this one. He'd had to hire another horse in Gallatin City to carry her travel boxes, as well as all of her new purchases.

There weren't many options for a woman here who wasn't dependent on her husband or father. Or she should say, a respectable woman. Since working in a brothel or serving drinks and dancing in a saloon were not acceptable options to her, J.B. had offered other suggestions. Cook, laundress, seamstress. She was a poor cook and a merely adequate seamstress (which J.B. had assured her would not be a terrible hindrance in this neck of the woods). Nor did she have funds to invest in a mine or stock lumber for a lumberyard.

She'd wanted to wait until they arrived in Virginia City to make her decision. She wanted to see the city and maybe it would help her choose her path. But J.B. had nixed that idea.

"It's a long way to get supplies if you can't get what you want in Virginia City," he said, shaking his head. J.B. had explained there were stores in Virginia City, but he couldn't be sure the supplies she'd need would be stocked, so it was best to make the decision and purchases while they could.

She'd opted for laundress.

On her family farm, she'd been in charge of the laundry since she was sixteen. Even after she'd married, she'd done laundry for herself, her husband, and any hired hands and migrant workers. It was hard work but she liked the sense of accomplishment that came from starting the day with dirty clothes and ending it with clean ones. She'd only had to do that once or twice a week, instead of six days, but now, she could keep her own income and decide how to spend it.

J.B. had taken her back to the ferry landing where a supplies boat had just landed. They negotiated to buy two tin tubs, an iron boiling pot, boxes of borax and starch, two irons, lye soap, rope, and wooden clothes pegs. That had taken nearly the last of her funds. She was grateful that J.B. hadn't asked her for money to hire the second horse needed to haul her travel boxes and the new supplies.

J.B. offered to let her set up on his plot, since there was a small spring bringing in fresh water nearby, with deferred rent in return for getting his own clothes washed by her. She'd gone from prospective bride to prospecting laundress in a matter of days.

So, here she was, riding along behind a man she barely knew, more dependent on him than he even realized.

"I think you ought to know that I am nearly out of money."

J.B. turned his head to look over his shoulder at Delia. She could feel the red heat in her cheeks. They were approaching the end of their first day's travel, with one more ahead of them the next day. She'd pretty much guaranteed that unless J.B. was rotten to the core, he had no choice but to keep helping her. He grunted and said, "I'll help you out until you're on your feet." Then, he faced forward again, but she heard him mumble, "We'll make Cal pay us back."

THE SECOND DAY, THE TRAIL THEY TRAVELED ALONG THE RIVER opened up into a long, broad valley. Mountains surrounded it. It was so beautiful that Delia pushed her bonnet off and let it hang down her back. She didn't want to miss any of the scenery, even if she was getting too much color from the intense sun. The valley was straw colored, except along the Madison River, where the deep blue water was riffled with white breaks and the green grasses and leafy trees.

Delia watched a bald eagle swoop along the water and rise with a fish in its talons, carrying it off to a nest in a tall cottonwood tree.

The valley turned brown and pine green as it marched through the foothills and up into the mountains.

J.B. pointed. "This is the Madison Range. That's the Gravelly Range, and over there, those are the Tobacco Root Mountains."

Delia pointed to one mountain. "That white bit over there? Is that snow? In August?"

J.B.'s voice carried over his shoulder as he guided the horses forward. "Yes. There's some spots up on the mountaintop that keep their snow all winter here. It's hard to imagine, considering how hot we are down here right now."

Delia merely nodded. Hard to imagine, indeed.

As they headed across the valley toward Gravelly Range, Delia thought the hillside in the distance was moving. They were so far away, though, she couldn't tell what she was seeing.

"Are those buffalo?" she asked excitedly.

"Elk," responded J.B. "See those lighter spots? That's the hind end of the elk. Like a white-tailed deer, but much bigger."

As they got closer, the details became clearer. The elk were bigger, and had bigger necks, thicker shoulders. The racks on the bulls were massive. One of them called out, a bugle like nothing Delia had heard before. She realized she was grinning as she rode along behind J.B. It was different seeing the country on horseback, instead of speeding at thirty-five miles per hour in a train, or in a boat, unable to travel off the water path.

They passed the elk and headed up a trail. It was afternoon. It was hot. Sweat gathered along both their backs. She tried to lean back, away from J.B.'s damp shirt.

Finally, after several ups and downs, they reached a lookout. In front of them was a narrow v-shaped valley, pressed between the hills they'd just crossed and more hills leading to yet another mountain range. It was Alder Gulch.

J.B. halted the horses. "Those are the Ruby Mountains across there." He pointed. "And this is Virginia City." Below them was a creek, pressed in on both sides by dozens of shacks, cabins and tents. The ground was torn up everywhere they looked, the creek bordered by piles of rock and dirt. The hillsides around the town were nearly naked.

"Where are the trees?" Delia asked cautiously. "Shouldn't there be lots of Alder trees?"

"Not many now. Most have been cut down for cabins and sluice boxes and the like."

"Sluice boxes?"

"It's a long narrow box. You run water over your slag and hope to find gold."

"Is that what you do?"

"No, I have a pit mine. I dig, run the ore through my rocker box."

Delia felt like he was speaking a foreign language. She felt she was looking at a foreign country. There were a dozen popup mining towns, having existed for less than three years, along this ten-mile stretch of Alder Creek. Ten thousand men were crammed into these shantytowns. Cabins and tents, shacks and lean-tos, anything to allow them to stay and mine for a better future.

And she was going to live here with them.

CHAPTER 8

Delia couldn't believe her eyes. Seeing Virginia City up close was even stranger than seeing it from above. She came from a small town, and she'd seen some really small ones on her way out West, including Gallatin City. She had even seen some big towns along the way.

Independence, Missouri was a staging point for travelers and there were hundreds of pioneers suiting up. Fort Benton, with its soldiers and ferry station goers was impressively full of hubbub. But this took the cake. It was a small town with the population of a big one.

Spreading up the hills and down to the river were dozens of buildings that looked hastily built. Some cabins were only part built, and then the rest, including the upper walls and roof, were made of canvas. There were wagons with grass growing around the wheels, clearly being used as homes. Tents.

There were random holes in the ground where someone had decided to dig for gold. Down by the creek, looking past some buildings, Delia could see the rocks and dirt that had been dug up.

The dirt track that was the main road was bordered by small cabins with false fronts.

The fronts and, in a few spots, boardwalks made it look bigger and more familiar. Some businesses, like the new wagon and blacksmith, didn't even have a building. They were conducting business out in the open.

Delia had never seen so many muddy, dirty men in her life. It was late afternoon and many of them were returning from a day's work. There were clear signs of army veterans, encamped with their former comrades. Skinny, ragged Southerners gave the stink eye to skinny, slightly less ragged Northerners. Two men broke out in a brawl not ten feet from her. The war was over, but it didn't seem to matter to these men.

There were drunk men and sober men, sad sacks and cheering groups. It was a strange microcosm of the world, with barely any women. Heads swiveled as she and J.B. rode down the trodden road. She sat behind him on the horse, her arms around his waist. She could hear them. "A woman!" "Look at that gal!" "Think she's going to Big Bertha's?"

And so here she was, riding through town and drawing so much attention that she felt Lady Godiva couldn't have had more eyes upon her.

Suddenly, she thought she saw someone she recognized. She lurched her head around to get a better look, but the man had turned off behind a group of tents and she lost sight of him.

"Whoa, Delia, are you falling off?" asked J.B.

"Oh, no, I'm sorry," she mumbled, still craning her neck. "I saw my husband. I mean, a man who looks like him."

"You're holding me pretty tight. Are you sure you're alright?" She stopped craning and faced forward again, and loosened her fingers, which had indeed been grasping J.B.'s sides tightly. J.B. took her silence and applied his own interpretation.

"It must be hard to be reminded of your husband and your loss."

She wanted to change the subject and decided not to be subtle about it. "You said there were a lot of men here, but it's a bit overwhelming to see so many, and to not see any women."

His next words both concerned and reassured her. "There are many more men working the placer mines. And there are a few women here, some helping husbands with mine work, some off preparing meals, etc. A few work in the saloons and..." he paused to cough, "other places. The ones who don't want undue attention, try to keep a low profile. You'll see them at church on Sunday."

Just then, they passed a rather decent-looking log cabin with a tiny, neat yard in front of it. A number of men were standing around it, looking at her hopefully. When they had put the lot behind them, Delia thought she heard a round of groans.

"What just happened?" she asked.

J.B. didn't turn to look at her when he said, "That was Big Bertha's. It's...a brothel. Begging your pardon, but I believe those fellows were hoping that was your destination."

What could she possibly say to that? Her face burned and she was glad J.B. couldn't see it.

J.B.'s cabin was toward the outskirts of Virginia City. He led the horse off the main road, away from the creek, a short distance, turned again onto a secondary road, and quickly stopped in front of a cabin. Delia slid off the back of the horse, wishing she could soak her sore muscles back in that hot spring they visited the day before. While J.B. tied the horses to the railing at his front door, she looked around. The cabin was made of hewn logs that crisscrossed at the corners, packed with mud or clay. There were two windows with shutters over them. There was a low-peaked roof with a chimney peeking out. This building was beginning to silver, but like most everything else she'd seen, it was clearly a fairly new building.

Along the left side there was a dusty path, about three feet wide, heading up the hill toward other cabins, some of which were half built right into the hills. On the right side was a narrow yard shared with another cabin. J.B. had said she could live and work here, but Delia wasn't sure where?

J.B. unloaded one box, the one Cal had asked her to bring out, and carried it into the cabin. She followed him. Inside, the main room took up the left two thirds of the building. There was a cook-stove and dry sink, a bucket near the door for bringing water, a simple table and two chairs. A third side of the table had a log set along it like a bench. There was a small window that would overlook the path Delia had seen.

J.B. opened the shutters and warm sunlight beamed in. The second, smaller room on the right, held two bunks, one above the other, on one wall. The other side of the room was stacked with boxes and supplies, J.B. explained, that J.B. and Cal, when he was in town, used for mining. A couple of hooks were on the wall for clothes, and that was it. The whole building, tiny as it was, was set up with the compact efficiency of a Conestoga wagon.

After showing Delia the cabin, J.B. took her outside to the path that ran alongside. J.B. pointed to another—even smaller —trail that led to a spring. Someone had dug out the hummock and lined it with rocks, creating a steady stream. Flat rocks lined the ground around it, allowing a place to rest a bucket and a way to avoid the mud. The runoff quickly joined a tiny creek that headed down toward the larger Alder Creek.

Next, J.B. pointed to a small shack fifteen feet behind his cabin. "There is where you can sleep and you can run your business in this yard." He gestured to the space between the two buildings.

The shack was a hodgepodge of a stacked stone foundation

that merged into the gentle slope of the hillside, its stick walls covered with black tarpaper and, thankfully, an actual shingled roof. A door stood in the center of the front wall and there was a small shuttered window to its left.

Delia looked around the yard. She could set up tubs along the side of the cabin, haul water from the spring, and run lines to dry between the two cabins. She could make it work.

Inside, the shack was empty.

"We were just finishing this. We planned to put in a stove and table, a few bunks to rent out. There are a lot of men looking for places to sleep. I'll finish it up for you."

"Oh," said Delia. She was terribly inconveniencing this man. "J.B., I'm sorry. You could get so much more rent from six men. Perhaps I should find somewhere else to live..." She looked around, as though a solution would appear.

"Delia, this is until Cal comes back to work things out with you. It'll be just fine."

She nodded. She didn't have any money to rent somewhere else anyway. She looked around the room again.

"If you can put a high board here, I can do some of my ironing inside."

"Well, heating those irons might be a problem. We ordered the stove but it hasn't arrived yet. It's supposed to get here before winter closes down the roads from Utah."

From what she'd seen so far, many men wouldn't care about whether their clothes were ironed, but some might. "I suppose you wouldn't mind if I used your stove until then?"

She felt she should feel awkward about going into a man's house to heat her irons (that made her blush) but somehow, it didn't. He treated her with such respect, it was the home of her self-proclaimed "fiancé," and this crazy town didn't seem to warrant getting too wrapped up in social expectations. She only hoped that her stove arrived before winter set in.

"Not a problem. I'm guessing you'll want a fire pit for

heating your wash water." He flung out his arm to gesture out the door to the yard. Delia couldn't help it. She flinched.

J.B. looked right at her, startled. He hesitated and she looked away, praying he wouldn't say anything. Her reaction – her reasons for it – was not something she wanted to discuss.

He let his arm drop. "I'll get on the fire pit and a workbench tomorrow. But it's getting into evening now. I'll get the bunk set up right now. I've got some lumber stacked along the far side of my cabin."

Delia realized how much this man was doing for her, and how much trouble she'd have had if left on her own. "Thank you, J.B. Thank you." She wanted to reach out and touch him, rest her hand on his arm, even hold his hand. After riding for two days with him, leaned upon his back, she felt like it should be okay to touch him, to feel that closeness again.

And that made her stop herself. What good could come of creating a greater intimacy between them? Plus, she could tell that behaving as though she was engaged to Calvin, to his friend, made her off-limits. She appreciated a man who valued his friendship and the engagement.

She watched him build the bunk as she unpacked her few belongings. When he finished, he got up off the floor and she saw him flinch, as though pinched in his stump. He stood back and looked at the flat wood bunk, attached to the wall on one side and supported by two legs on the other. She saw his brow furrow and he turned and left. *Well,* she thought to herself, *I guess he's had enough of me – and the troubles I bring.* She felt bereft.

Suddenly, J.B. was back. He carried an odd-shaped fabric bag. Only when he lay it on the bunk and began to punch the bag into shape did she realized it was a straw mattress. *His* straw mattress, the one he usually slept on. A quick flash of a sleeping J.B. crossed her mind. She felt her face flame.

J.B. turned and saw her blushing face. "Uh. Um. This is from Cal's bunk. It's not been used too much, but we'll get some fresh straw and you can make your own mattress tomorrow."

It wasn't his. It was Calvin's. But she couldn't explain her mistake. And it didn't really matter.

"I'm sorry."

He quirked a brow.

"I've put you out of your way. In so many ways. I…" She couldn't express how very aware she was of her dependency on him, and of how his helping her was saving her life. "Thank you. From the bottom of my heart."

He nodded. "You're welcome."

J.B. tipped his hat to her and then turned to leave. At the door, he paused; without looking back, he said, "Delia, no more apologies. Agreed?"

And he left. But this time, she didn't feel bereft.

CHAPTER 9

Delia poked at the smoldering ashes. She was trying to heat up more water, but she'd let the fire get too low. She was used to working on a stove, not an open fire. Heating up water was harder and took more time this way.

Before he'd left to go work his mine this morning, J.B. had assured her that she'd get the hang of it. She knew that was true, but it wasn't an advantage yet. She grabbed a couple of small sticks and stuck them in the coals. While she waited for them to catch, she grabbed her other stick that wasn't covered with ashes and stuck it in the tub piled with clothes. She swirled it around and the brown water showed how dirty the men's clothes were. Besides J.B.'s, two other men had spotted her setting up in the yard first thing in the morning and brought their clothes straightaway.

It looked like she'd have to rinse the miners' clothes, then wash them with soap, then rinse again. She couldn't imagine how else she'd get them clean. Delia rolled up her sleeves. She pulled an empty tub over and set about lifting the wet clothes out of the first tub and into the second. Then, she dragged the tub full of brown water to the edge of the yard. She grabbed one side and prepared to tip it.

"Stop right there!" A loud voice called out.

Delia dropped the edge of the tub and spun around. A woman was standing in the yard. She wore a mauve skirt and white blouse, appropriate for visiting in the day…anywhere but Montana Territory. She was attractive; with silky-looking brown hair piled on her head…a little too formal for Virginia City. Delia had a suspicion…

"I apologize for scaring you, Mrs. Watson." The woman didn't wait for Delia to respond. She stuck out her hand. "How do you do? I am Mrs. Bertha Banks."

Delia looked at the hand held out to her, and then at her own wet, dirty one.

"Oh, no bother," the woman said with a smile. "Now, you mustn't dump that water."

Delia looked back at the tub of dirty water. "Mrs. Banks?" she said timidly. She'd never spoken with a woman of ill repute before. She'd been raised to believe such a fallen woman would be obviously devilish, but this woman was friendly and gracious. Well, except for the yelled command that started the conversation.

"Call me Big Bertha. Everybody does," she said.

Delia noted that one aspect of Big Bertha that she could see warranted the nickname "Big." But then, the woman offered a brilliant smile and Delia thought, *Well, two.*

Big Bertha leaned in toward Delia and said in a quieter voice, "Gold, my dear. Gold."

That got Delia's attention. "I didn't notice any gold."

"You'll have to pan for it, dear. All the gold dust gets on the miner's clothes. You can collect it in the wash water. You'd be surprised how quickly it adds up. The Chinese launderers all do it in the California mining towns. I saw it when I was there. You should, too."

Delia looked back at the dirty water yet again. It seemed a crazy notion, but she had a feeling this woman was being straight. She wiped her hands on her apron and held one out. "Thank you, Bi- Big…Mrs. Banks. I'd hate to throw out the baby with the bathwater."

"You are more than welcome, my dear." Big Bertha spun around then, taking in the yard, the tubs, the sopping clothes, and even the mud clinging to the hem of Delia's dress. "Now, I've come to discuss business with you."

"Laundry?" Delia asked. She couldn't help but notice that her dress had several inches of mud coating the bottom of it, while Bertha's skirts barely had a dusting along the hem. Bertha's hemline, Delia suddenly realized, was shorter than her own. Was it to avoid dragging in the dirt, or to show off her ankles?

Big Bertha shook her head. "No, dear. Now, please don't take offense, but I hear you had other plans when you came out here." She waved her hand at the laundry tubs as she spoke. "If this doesn't suit, I have a business that might interest you. It's not so…labor intensive."

This woman was afraid she'd offend Delia by bringing up her missing fiancé, but not by suggesting Delia turn to whoring? How did one respond to such an offer? It was not one Delia had ever thought would come her way. She knew she ought to be offended, but instead she was fighting a smile. It felt weird on her face and she suspected it was half grimace. "No. No. I…uh…thank you…no."

Big Bertha assessed Delia for a moment and, with the barest of grins, bowed her head in acknowledgement. "Very well. If you ever change your mind…"

Delia shook her head. Just then, a movement behind Bertha caught her eye. Delia looked over Bertha's shoulder down the path past J.B.'s cabin, down to the road. She saw that horrible man Freddy that had accosted her in Gallatin City. He looked just as greasy as before, but he wasn't smiling and acting friendly like that first time. He was standing there watching Delia with intent, unblinking, snake eyes. She felt a wave of revulsion. Bertha spun around and upon seeing Freddy, she called out with a wave of her hands, "Shoo. Go on now." Freddy's lip curled up and he slunk off.

The two women watched for a moment longer, waiting to see if Freddy reappeared. When he didn't, they turned away from the road. Bertha glanced over at J.B.'s cabin. "You're lucky, you know. Mr. Wood is a war hero. Not many men will give him and his any trouble." Delia was about to disclaim being "his", but Bertha continued their previous conversation as though they hadn't been interrupted. "Now, I hope you will feel free to call on me if you ever need the assistance of a friend. There are not many females around here and we need to stick together."

Delia couldn't help but smile, a real one this time. "I appreciate that greatly."

"There's a boy, young Kit, who hangs around the edge of my yard. He usually knows where to find me. You can relay a message to me through him any time."

"Oh, yes, right." Delia felt foolish. It hadn't even occurred to her that to call on Big Bertha meant calling on a brothel.

As though she could read Delia's mind, Big Bertha chuckled. "Good luck, my dear. Have a nice day!" She sashayed out of the yard.

Without Big Bertha, the yard had lost some color. Delia picked up her stick and poked at the fire. It was out. She'd have to start again, but it didn't seem so onerous this time. It was nice to meet another woman. And, she was excited to ask J.B. how to get that gold out of the tub.

CHAPTER 10

When Delia opened her cabin door, she found J.B. hard at work under the morning sky. To the east, the low-lying yellow sun was chasing pale blue toward the purple of the last of the night sky. To the west, a few stars still shone.

J.B. was stacking stones around her wash fire ashes. She admired his broad shoulders, his shirt straining under the weight of the stones he was lifting.

"Good morning, J.B.," she said, drawing her shawl closer around.

"Good morning, Delia," he replied. His breath steamed in the crisp air. It was hard to believe they'd be roasting later that afternoon.

She walked around to look more carefully at his project. "What are you doing?"

He finished arranging a stone, the last one, and then looked over at Delia with a smile. "Isn't it obvious? I'm building you a fire ring. Your fire didn't bank overnight, and from the look of the kindling pile, you had to restart your fire a couple of times yesterday anyway."

Delia felt a warm glow inside her. This man was so thoughtful. And then he spoke again.

"I'll have to spend more time looking for kindling than gold if you can't figure out how to keep a fire going." He finished with a smirk.

The warm glow sputtered. She put her hands on her hips. "You…You're a rascal," she said, half amused, half exasperated.

Then J.B. pointed a toe at the two tubs full of dirty water. "Do you need help emptying those?"

Delia nearly jumped. She darted forward, placing herself between J.B. and the tubs. "No!"

He looked at her warily.

"I wanted to ask you last night, but you got home late and I was so very tired I went to bed early. I want to pan for gold. Will you teach me?"

J.B.'s brows drew down. "The wash water?"

"Oh, yes," said Delia excitedly. "The gold dust washes off the clothes and I can pan for it. If you'll show me." She smiled eagerly.

J.B. shook his head, not in dismissal but at the vagaries of life. "Now that is something I never considered. Where'd you learn about that?"

Delia tried to keep her face neutral, but she was looking forward to J.B.'s reaction. She tried to sound casual. "From my new friend, Big Bertha."

J.B. froze in place except his jaw, which dropped open. Delia peeled with laughter. She had liked Bertha more the more she thought about their encounter the day before. She equally liked teasing J.B., too.

Delia grabbed J.B.'s hand and drew him over to stand before the tubs. "Bertha said the Chinese launderers pan for gold. I ran my hands round the bottom of the tubs, and I can feel some sand and grit, but what little I could pull out with my fingers didn't seem to have any gold in it. I don't know if there's none here, or I'm doing it wrong. I'm not actually panning, I know." She took a breath and kept going. "I know it's silly, but the idea of finding my own gold, even gold dust, is so exciting. Will you teach me, J.B.?"

J.B.'s shocked expression turned to alarm. Delia realized she was hanging off his arm, wringing his hand. She let go and stepped back, nearly tripping into the nearer tub. J.B. grabbed her arm. He shook his head again, and she found she was growing to dislike that gesture of his. She regained her balance and then slipped her arm free.

"Not a problem," she said. "There's plenty of miners who'll be happy to help me, I'm sure." She walked over to the side of her cabin and lifted her apron off a hook. "Thank you for the fire ring. You have a good day digging." She busied herself with tying the ribbon behind her back. She knew from experience when she had created a perfect bow. Then, she gently tugged on one tail so that one loop was a little smaller than the other.

J.B. looked from Delia to his knapsack with his tools and supplies for the day. She didn't like that his mining was more important than her, which was rather unfair, she acknowledged to herself. But she didn't want to acknowledge it to him. She took a page from Bertha's book. She threw out her hands in a shooing motion. "Go on, then."

Her sour mood turned quickly at the offended look on J.B.'s face. He clearly did not like being shooed out of his own yard. Delia couldn't help but laugh, which confused him further. But she had suddenly seen the ludicrousness of arguing over sticking a pan in a tub of dirty water and hoping fortune would smile.

"Truly, J.B. I'll manage. Go on to your mine. I can see it's where you want to be." She smiled and hoped he realized how genuine her olive branch was.

J.B. shifted his weight from one foot to the other, back and forth, and once again Delia had the feeling she was a wild animal that J.B. feared would attack. Finally, he stopped, and said, "I'll help you. You're going to need to do it now if you want to be able to do any other washing today." Given how dirty the tub water was, Delia couldn't argue with that.

Instead of reaching into his knapsack, J.B. entered his cabin and quickly came back out with a tin pan, round, with sloping sides, but fairly flat. He handed it to Delia.

"Don't you take this to your mine?"

"No," he said, as he rolled up his sleeves. "This is for gold panning – in the water. I do hard rock mining. I've got my pick ax, my shovel, and my rocker box for most of my work. Now, come over here and I'll show how to use this." He took the pan back from her.

Delia imagined using the pan to scoop water out of the tub. She'd look in the water for gold…and then what? There had to be more to it than that.

J.B. held the pan flat between his two hands. He reached into the tub and scooped up some of the sandy silt from the bottom along with the water. Holding the pan under the water, he moved it forward and back, forward and back. Then, he carefully lifted it out of the water and began to swirl it in a circle. Occasionally, he'd pour off a little water.

"Won't the gold dust get poured out?" Delia asked, even though, peering over J.B.'s arms, she couldn't see anything that looked like gold.

He gave a small shake of his head, but kept swirling in a clockwise motion, his eyes glued on the pan. "You see, gold, in general, is heavier than everything else in the pan. Even the gold dust is heavier than the water. It'll collect…" he paused to point, "…here, where the sides of the pan are joined to the base, along this edge." He returned to swirling and pouring. Finally, he stopped and reached into the pan and pinched out a tiny grain of gold. He held it out on his fingertip, to Delia. The morning sun rising behind them shone and caused it to glint. She held out her own finger and J.B. carefully pressed his to hers, until it stuck to her fingertip. She gazed at in awe. Here she was, in a city devoted to discovering gold. She had this teeny tiny particle, but still felt a wave of excitement and hope crash through her. This. This was why people gave up all comforts in hope. In hope.

They were both leaning over her gold-tipped finger. She smiled at J.B. He smiled back at her. She whispered, "What do I do with it?"

He whispered back, "You collect it, and more like it. I'll give you a poke bag. When you have enough, we'll take it the assayers office for weighing. For now, do you have a handkerchief you can wrap it in?"

Delia nodded and then began walking to the cabin. She held her finger out in front of her, not taking her eyes off the little spot of gold. She moved slowly, lest she create a wind that would blow her new fortune away. Inside the cabin she used one hand to carefully lay out her kerchief. She placed the grain of gold in the middle, folded it up precisely, and tucked it into a jar which she placed on the shelf. Once completed, she heard a voice behind her.

"If you move any slower, it'll be yesterday." J.B. had followed her and stood in the doorway, waiting. "Why don't you come back over and try panning by yourself, before I leave? Make sure it sticks."

Delia was too excited to take issue with his quip about her speed. She slid by J.B. and rushed back to the tub. She rolled up her sleeves and then grabbed the pan, plunging it into the water. She held it underwater like J.B. had, and swirled it about. Suddenly, J.B. reached over and placed his hand on her wrist, stopping her.

"Hold on, Delia! You're not stirring up lemonade. Go back

and forth, back and forth." He tried to move her hand, but they weren't in sync. He started to reach his other arm around her, and then stopped. "Uh, may I?"

Delia gave a quick nod. He reached around her until his front was to her back, with both of his arms wrapped around her, his hands on her wrists. She couldn't help but blush.

"Like this," he said, gently pushing her hands forward, and then pulling them back. He created a rhythm, occasionally murmuring, "Back and forth." She felt his warm breath on her neck. A little shiver ran down her spine.

"Now, raise the pan out of the water," he murmured in her ear. She raised the pan up, pouring some water off the side.

"Hold it level," he added. "Now, swirl." With his hands on her wrists, he helped her establish a rhythm of when to pour and when to swirl. It was a paradox. She would be able to do this without him, but with his arms around her she could barely focus enough to remember to move the pan around.

After a few minutes of swirling and peering, swirling and peering, they stopped to look for gold. They spotted two flecks of gold in the water, caught on the edge in the bottom of the pan. At first, she stared at them, thrilled to see the gold. But then, she was made aware again of J.B.'s arms around her, an unnatural stillness in him that told her he was as aware of their intimate position as she was.

"So, ah…I will…I can do this," she said, quietly. "Thank you, J.B."

She waited, and J.B. stayed as he was for a moment longer than she expected, longer than necessary. When he withdrew his arms from around her, she heard him expel a deep breath. She held the pan still, aware of him as he stepped back from her. Out the corner of her eye, she saw him unrolling his sleeves and buttoning them, fumbling. Finally, he grabbed his knapsack and hitched it over his shoulder. Before he left, he stood looking at her. Delia wondered what he was going to say.

"See you tonight," was all he said before turning and walking out the yard.

Delia focused on the two gold flecks in the pan. She carefully placed the pan on her wash table, preparing to claim her gold.

CHAPTER 11

J.B. sat at his table, ostensibly carving a block of wood, but in fact watching Delia. She stood in front of his stove frying up a ham steak and potatoes. Her hair was pulled back in a bun. Her cheeks and nose were red from spending the days in the sun. J.B. couldn't begin to acknowledge how much he appreciated coming home to a pretty woman cooking his supper, or how much he'd missed that sense of family that a woman brought.

Coming home after a day working his claim and sometimes finding Delia had finished up her work early and was cooking supper for them both…well, it was a fine surprise. They didn't have a regular schedule, but J.B. could see how easy it would be to fall into the routine of a married couple with her…except that they lived in separate cabins and she considered herself engaged to his friend. He couldn't decide if she actually believed Cal was coming back to marry her or not.

J.B. looked down at the wood block in his hand. He'd been out in Montana Territory for a little over a year helping to carve out a new world. He enjoyed the adventure of discovery and blazing a new path…even being a part of Manifest

Destiny. He was expanding the borders of the United States of America…bringing democracy and Christianity across the continent. At least, that's what he'd thought.

Now, watching Delia putter around the stove, he wondered if what he had wanted all along was simply to strike it rich so he could settle down and raise his own family in peace and prosperity. She came out West for a better life. Wasn't he doing the same?

Delia looked over and saw him watching. She offered a gentle smile. "It's ready."

She took two plates off the shelf and loaded them with ham and potatoes. J.B. took his carving block and knife and placed them on the floor beside his chair. He brushed the wood shavings off the table. Delia placed the plates on the now empty table. She crossed the room to select a fork and knife for each of them.

J.B. looked at the line of her back. From the moment he met her, he'd seen that she was a sturdy farm girl, but now after even just a short time, it appeared she was getting stronger from carrying buckets and scrubbing clothes. Her slender frame moved with strength and grace.

She came back and sat down across from J.B. She reached over to place his fork and knife next to his plate. The fork slipped and clattered against the plate, a jarring noise after the peaceful silence they'd been enjoying.

Delia's eyes flew to his face. "Oh! I'm sorry! I'm…" She slowly pulled her hand back to her side of the table.

"Not a problem," J.B. said, picking up the fork and knife. He began to cut his steak, as though nothing was amiss. But inside, he seethed. It wasn't very Christian of him, but he was glad her husband was dead.

CHAPTER 12

Delia pushed back a hank of damp hair from her forehead. It was early, and still cool out. There even remained some frost hiding in the shadows, so unlike any late August that she'd ever experienced before. But over the washtub of warm water, which sat on her workbench, and next to the fire heating up the boiler pot, the air was warm and wet. The morning sun reflected off the wash water and blinded Delia. She turned her head away and realized with a start that a man and a dog were standing in the yard, not ten feet from her.

As her eyes adjusted, she saw an older man of middle height and considerable grime smiling at her. His brown hair, tanned and grubby face, and soiled clothes gave him a consistently brown coloring from head to toe. Only his teeth and the whites of his eyes were lighter. But his smile was charming and his cheeks dimpled.

The dog didn't have dimples but did tilt its head in a way that was charming for a dog. He was little, with wiry brown and white hair.

"Pardon me, Ma'am," the man said. "I've just returned to

town from an extended expedition and I heard you're taking in laundry." He shifted the armload of clothes he had pinned against his side. "I'm in desperate need," he added with a waggle of his brow.

Delia couldn't help but smile. She was glad for the business, but equally glad for the good spirits of this man.

"Put your linens over there," she said, pointing to a basket on the ground next to her table. As he walked over to do that, she wiped her hands on her apron. The dog followed, sniffing all around.

"I'm Mrs. Watson."

"And I'm Charles Chatsworth Dawson, but folks call me "Chatty.""

"Nice to meet you, Chatty."

"Is there a Mr. Watson?"

Delia wanted to groan. The men always asked. She repeated her line. "My fiancé is out of town but he'll be along."

"Are you marrying J.B., then? Now why's he off gallivanting when his lady is here alone? Though I imagine he has so many fellows that'd protect you with their own lives, after what he did in the war for them, that you're plenty safe."

"No, sir, not J.B." Delia had heard a few references to J.B.'s time in the War Between the States, but he wasn't willing to talk it about with her. She was tempted to ask Chatty but didn't want to encourage personal inquiries. To stave off more questions, she said, "I expect I can have your wash done and dried by…" Delia paused a moment to check the sky for rain clouds. There rarely were any, but force of habit kept her checking. "By day after tomorrow."

Chatty nodded his acceptance of the schedule, but he didn't leave. He stood there, surveying the hanging lines, washtubs, and boiler pot and then Delia again.

"It's a real pleasure to see a feminine face in these parts. Especially such a pretty one."

Delia gave a small nod of thanks. She'd become accustomed to the compliments of the men of Virginia City and rarely even blushed anymore. There were so few women that somehow, she reminded every man of some special girl back home. Chatty's compliment felt genuine and kind, and not lecherous like some of the men. Even so, she turned back to her wash.

But still he didn't leave.

"Yup, I've been leading a group over to this area that has lots of geysers and mudpots. Very unusual landscape," said Chatty. Delia glanced up and he nodded his head as though responding to a question from her.

"Not many people over that-a-ways," he continued, "but more and more since Colter first explored it."

Delia couldn't help it. She usually didn't encourage the men to hang around, but washing clothes was not a job to take up her mind like it took up her hands. And this man had a way of talking; like a born storyteller. "Colter?" she asked, standing behind her washboard, scrubbing slowly so the slosh of the water didn't drown out Chatty's voice.

"You don't know John Colter?" he exclaimed. She shook her head. "Oh, Mrs. Watson, what a man he was. He came west with the Lewis and Clark expedition, but never left. Hunter, trapper, guide. An all-around man. Even good for negotiating with the Indians." He leaned over to peer into the tub where she was heating clean water. It was just starting to give off little wisps of steam. "Well, except that one time." His eyes slid over to hers and the twinkle told her he was just waiting for her to take the bait.

Delia pulled the shirt she was scrubbing out of the tub and twisted it to squeeze out the water. She took her time, pretending she wasn't curious about "that one time." Finally, she dropped it into a tub of clean water.

"Alright," she said as she grabbed the next shirt to be scrubbed. "You've got me wondering. What happened to this John Colter?"

That's all it took to get Chatty chatting. He spun the tale of John Colter, canoeing down a river with his partner. "He was 'round forty years, give or take, back in 1808." With his light-hearted voice Delia could picture in her mind the two men looking for beavers to trap. Then, they encountered a band of Blackfeet braves. Chatty described how Colter was disarmed and stripped naked.

Delia blushed. This wasn't the kind of story she was used to back home. Chatty's voice turned serious when he described how the partner was shot, and then shot again, to death, when he didn't do as told. But then his voice lightened again, when he told how the Blackfeet told Colter to start running. And so, the naked man did, as fast as he could while they chased him.

"And finally, he dove into the river and came up inside a beaver lodge." Chatty nodded. "Yup. He grabbed the beaver by the tail, told it to scooch, and stayed there till the coast was clear."

Delia realized she was sitting back on her heels, the wet shirt motionless in her hands, dripping down the washboard.

"And then?"

"And then he had a long walk back to civilization. Naked." Chatty waggled his brows again and Delia laughed.

"You spin a yarn like no one I know," she said with a smile that wouldn't come off her face. "You should rent a hall and collect fees."

Chatty looked startled, and for the first time since she met him, a little less confident. "Thank you kindly, Mrs. Watson."

Chatty looked around the yard once more.

"Well, I'd better be moving along. I can see you have plenty to keep you busy. I'll be seeing you day-after." He tipped his hat to Delia. "Now, where's that dog of mine?"

Delia heard a slurping noise and looked under the table. The little dog was lying there with her bar of lye soap between his front paws. He was gnawing on it like bone.

"Oh, you! Shoo! Little devil! Go on!" she stomped her foot at the dog and he took off running out of the yard. He dropped the soap half way there. Chatty picked it up and handed her the dirty, dog-slobbered, tooth-marked bar.

"Apologies, Mrs. Watson," he said.

She watched Chatty walk out of the yard and turn south down the road. Back home, it would have been considered an inappropriate – or certainly questionable – story for a young woman. Colter's story would have been censored – *unclothed*, it might have been whispered, at best. Delia loved the freedom of Montana Territory. It was hard living, but it was her own choice of living. She was glad she had come here, even though things hadn't worked out as she planned. The problem was, would she keep going like this forever?

She thought about J.B. and Cal. She was letting J.B. think that she was hoping Cal would change his mind. But she knew he wouldn't. She could tell by the way Cal had talked about the woman he was helping. He was smitten and that woman would be three kinds of foolish if she didn't respond in kind.

Delia shook her head and pushed the shirt down into the water. The warm water lapped around her wrists. But she let J.B. think she was still hoping for Cal because it kept him, and others, from hoping for more. After the gold panning lesson, though, she wondered if her wall was crumbling.

She'd been willing to take a risk with Cal, before she'd seen him, when he wasn't a real man, but a boy from her memories. But now he was a real person. And so were J.B. and Chatty and all the men she'd met. How could she tell them, and especially J.B., the truth – that she wasn't sure she was a widow?

CHAPTER 13

SEPTEMBER 1865

J.B. trudged down the road through town, glad to be headed home. The sun was just kissing the tops of the mountains but it was still nice and warm out. It was nicer than that morning, when a frost had covered the ground and nipped at his ears. He was pushing himself hard, trying to get as much out of his mine as he could before the cold weather set in. While he wouldn't be halted by ice like the placer miners that worked the creeks, even hard rock mining became unbearably hard when the ground froze.

He looked up at the sun again. It was September, and already the sun was setting earlier and rising later. He had till November or so before things ground to a halt. He'd seen wagons and stagecoaches taking men down to Utah already. Men who had spent the summer living under wagons and bushes, or with sheets hung off tree branches instead of even a tent. Men who couldn't survive the winter that way.

He wondered what the winter would bring for Delia. Laundry still needed to be done, but even that would slow down. Even the army had cut the frequency of clothes washing down in the winter to only twice a week. He had grown to appreciate her presence, a brief balm of femininity in the masculine barrens of the mining town. She didn't discuss Cal, except to claim he'd be along as soon he was able and then they'd be married. Sometimes, J.B. wondered if she really believed that, but he couldn't imagine why she'd bother with the claim if she didn't. Sometimes, he felt she liked *him* too, but always she had her wall up against J.B.

J.B. looked up, knowing he'd see the intersection that led to his road as he walked round the bend. As usual, more fellows than usual in a regular town were walking by or standing and chatting in the street. It took a moment for J.B. to realize they were all gathered in front of the blacksmith and wagon shop and all facing in the same direction.

As he came up on the crowd, he saw what they were looking at. It seemed more than a few men thought watching Delia do just about anything was the best view around. In this case, she was standing over by the anvil, just past the post and rail fence of the small corral, with her back to the road, conversing with the blacksmith. She was making motions with her hands and J.B. figured she was describing something for the blacksmith to make.

He looked back at the gawkers.

There were short guys and tall ones, skinny ones and even one heavyset one. And—that damn Freddy hanging out. He was talking with the heavy fellow, but both were looking into the yard at Delia. J.B. quickened his pace, ignoring the ache in his bad foot, but as soon as he was noticed, the men scattered, all of them. A few passed J.B., tipping their hats to him, but the rest turned tail and walked away. One fellow only walked five feet and then paused. At J.B.'s glare, the man pointed over his shoulder at a little cabin. "I…I live here."

Freddy tried to swagger past him, but J.B. reached out and

grabbed him by the collar. He backed the roughneck up against the side of stick and canvas shack, pushing the whole wall inward. "You've got no call to be pestering Mrs. Watson. I don't want to see you near her again."

Freddy smirked. "I was just thinking of asking her to do my laundry."

"Don't." J.B. twisted his fist, tightening the collar around Freddy's neck. "Or you'll be messing with me." He pulled around and shoved Freddy down the road, away from Delia's direction. "You better make tracks."

Delia might claim Cal as her fiancé, but most of the men around here recognized her as under J.B.'s protection. If Freddy hadn't figured that out on his own, he knew it now.

J.B. had known this would happen when Cal asked for his help, but he hadn't expected it to drag on this long. J.B. got all the responsibilities of a fiancée, without the benefits. Sure, they'd found a rhythm, living and working next to each other, which he enjoyed. But he worried…

He felt a tap on his shoulder. "J.B.?" It was Delia. J.B. was stunned by how lovely she looked. Once again, her bonnet was pushed back off her head, hanging down her back. Her face was sun-kissed and the hair around her face retained the curl it got from being around the steamy water all the time. Her green eyes sparkled and her smile was genuine.

He glared at her. She looked at him askance, but he wasn't going to explain his mood.

"Ah…I am having some strong hooks made so that I can hang some heavier things along the side of the cabin."

"I'll walk you home," he said brusquely. They turned off the main road and walked side by side up the hill toward the road that led them the short distance home.

When they arrived at his cabin, Delia paused to glance at him for only a moment before heading up the path toward the backyard. J.B. followed. He had nothing to say, or nothing he was willing to say, but he still didn't like leaving her presence. They entered the yard between the two buildings and saw, sitting on Delia's wash bench, a bushel basket filled with fresh-cut pine branches.

Delia spun back to him. "Oh, I almost forgot to thank you. I didn't even realize you were paying attention the other day, when I said I needed something to make a better-smelling soap. Thank you." She offered him a big smile.

"I didn't give you those branches." His mood was getting darker.

Delia looked startled. "A fellow brought them by earlier. He said 'my man' asked him to deliver them. I...I told him you weren't my man, but he just shrugged and left." She looked over at the basket. Was there a hint of disappointment in her face? He couldn't tell. Then she added, "I don't know who sent them, but I suppose I've discussed making a scented soap with several folk."

Delia walked to her hanging lines and began inspecting the clothes to see how dry they were. But J.B. was rooted in his spot. He was surprised by how much he resented some other man sending Delia flowers. Or at least, pine branches. He realized that he'd accepted Cal could come back and claim her after all, but J.B. wasn't sure he was willing to let anyone else do so.

CHAPTER 14

J.B. opened the shutter and looked out at the morning sky. The sun was just coming up. The sky was dark above, and even though the sun could not be seen beyond the mountains, the strong golden glow promised a warm day. This late in the season, the grasses were dormant, turned straw-colored, so he saw only yellows and shades of blue-gray in the world outside. A few stars still shone above.

J.B. stood there in his bare feet, buttoning his shirt, and inhaled deeply. He caught the scent of smoke, the many stove and campfires burning throughout the town. He saw a wisp of smoke drifting from behind his cabin across the path that ran under the window. Delia had just started a fire in her fire pit. Her pattern was to stoke the fire under the boiling pot she'd filled with water the night before. Then in the early morning light, after a quick sweep of her work area for tumbleweeds and anything else that might easily catch fire, she began hauling buckets of water from the creek to her rinse tub.

Just then, Delia emerged into view, holding two empty buckets and walking up the path to the spring. She was stronger, assuredly steadier and more confident with her loads than when she'd first arrived in Virginia City. She had no trouble carrying two full buckets of water now. Back in September, in the first few days when she'd struggled with one full bucket, he'd offered to help her haul them, but she had declined. "You have your mining. That's work enough for you. I have to do this on my own, to make this work." He'd seen the reason in this. After all, she couldn't depend on him to hang around all day scooping water.

He watched her skirts sway. He noticed she'd raised them a little. He caught glimpses of her ankles sometimes. He wasn't the only man who liked to watch her. Quite a few men were having her wash their laundry, and for some—he was quite sure—it was only an excuse to meet her. Some of these fellows hadn't cared to wash their clothes all summer until Delia arrived. At most, they'd gone and jumped in the river while still wearing them. And those fellows, they liked to hang around her.

Many a time, he'd seen her hand over the buckets to some lollygagger. She didn't seem to mind putting those men to work. So far as he could tell, heading off to their jobs became more appealing after she stopped talking. She wasn't rude, just focused on her own job. She did a good job, too. He'd come back at the end of the day to find the lines sagging under the weight of so many pants, long undergarments, shirts and socks.

Today, though, no one had yet arrived. J.B. ran his fingers through his hair, just starting to turn away from the window when he saw Delia trip and fall to the ground. He raced out of the log house and around the corner, bounding up the path at an awkward run-hop. "Are you alright, Delia?" He crouched down on one knee.

She brushed off her hands. "Oh, yes, I'm fine." She smiled that lovely smile at him, that genuine smile that reached her eyes and made him feel…well, something. She suddenly turned shy, looking down and brushing at her skirt. He stood up and held put his hand, preparing to help her rise.

"You ran out in your bare feet, just because I'm clumsy." She hesitated, looking at his scarred foot. J.B., not normally self-conscious, realized he didn't want Delia to think less of him. She didn't say anything but took his hand and rose to her feet. She shook out her skirt, the bottom of which was damp on one side from the spilled water. Luckily, most had spilled to the side, off the path. "You'd think I've walked this trail enough in the past week to know it by now."

He agreed with her. He scanned the ground to see what might have tripped her. He wanted to make sure she didn't fall again. There was a divot in the path, with sharp edges of dried dirt to indicate a rock had been removed recently. To the side of the path, he saw the matching rock, sharp-edged and aligned with the side of the path.

"Did you kick this rock loose? You must have stubbed your toe."

She was squeezing out the hem of her skirt. He caught a glimpse of her booted ankle.

"No, my toes are fine."

The rock had clearly been removed or knocked free very recently. J.B. leaned more heavily on his good foot. He looked along the path and saw several other divots, with the rocks moved carefully to create a border. "Well, it looks like one of your admirers wanted a smoother track for when he's hauling your water," said J.B., his eyes on the track. "He should have filled the holes."

It was then that he looked up from the ground and realized that Delia, in the process of smoothing out her skirt, had frozen. Her expression was…guarded, but something in her eyes, in her unmoving stance, expressed a deep fear.

"Delia? Delia?"

He reached forward to touch her shoulder, to wake her

from her trance. She jerked backward, so his hand was left grasping at air. "I should get back to work. Thank you." She grabbed her buckets and continued on to the spring. He could see her scanning the ground for more holes, but also glancing up, wary of something, or someone.

He watched her a moment and then turned to limp back to his cabin. Was she concerned about one of the men hanging around? He'd have to think about how he could help her, especially since she didn't seem to want his help. Did she think his foot made him incapable of helping her? He couldn't think of any concessions he'd made to his foot that she could have seen.

That question that popped into his mind frequently was burning his brain again. Was she still hoping to marry Cal? He wasn't sure of her plans, except that they didn't seem to include him in any role except landlord and friend.

For now, he'd put on his boots and head to the mine. He sure wished Cal would hurry up and fix his problem with that other gal. He needed his help with the mine and with Delia. He hadn't liked seeing her fall, more than he probably should care. But darn it all, he was concerned about her and didn't want to be.

He'd told himself after the war, he wouldn't take on that responsibility again. He just wanted to work his mine.

CHAPTER 15

Delia thought the clothes would never get as clean as they were getting today. She scrubbed a blue shirt along the washboard, over and over. She had such tension in her body that she felt only running or screaming might release it. And that was what she wanted to do, run and scream. The lye burned her skin, leaving it raw and chapped. She hated the soap, she thought, punctuating her angry thought with a slap of the shirt hitting the water.

She exchanged the blue shirt for a formerly cream-colored shirt and continued to hunch over the washboard. It was possible, as J.B. had said, that one of her bucket brigade had dug out those rocks in order to create a smoother path. It shouldn't upset her. It shouldn't.

But after what happened this morning, she couldn't help but think of her dead husband Steven, back in Missouri. This was something he'd done. He wanted the paths along their farm to be perfectly manicured. Any rocks or roots were clawed out. He'd place the rocks to the side of the path, making a border. He'd fill in the holes though. That was different.

She took a deep breath, recognizing her foolish fears. But now the memories were back, she couldn't stop them. Steven's uncle Geoffrey had told him that man's greatest achievement was to take control over nature. To run your farm with the precision of an army general was the ideal. Command your farm, your household, your family. "Let him have dominion…" Geoffrey would quote about a husband's role.

Steven took all of his uncle's exhortations to heart. Since his aunt, Geoffrey's wife, had passed away not long after Steven came to live with them, it had been just the two of them until she and Steven had married. She hadn't seen it when he courted her, but once married she saw how controlling both men were. They were two peas in a pod.

She remembered how angry he'd gotten at her when Uncle Geoffrey had said to him, "Is this how you run things?" at the sight of her kitchen garden, a bit weedier than it should have been. She knew he wouldn't defend her, telling his uncle she'd been under the weather with a cold. Instead, he'd pulled her aside, gripping her arm so hard she'd later found bruises.

"You're embarrassing me in front of Uncle!" Then he'd shoved her into the garden, where she weeded until the sun went down.

She'd worried about Steven's behavior, and their marriage. And then she'd worried in a different way, when he went off to war.

"Pardon me, Mrs. Watson?" She was startled to find a man close by. She was so lost in her thoughts, she couldn't seem to respond. She'd been so intent in her scrubbing and her memories that she hadn't noticed him. "J.B. told me you do a good job, but now I really believe. That shirt must be clean as new."

She looked down and wondered how long she'd been scrubbing this one shirt. But the tension was broken. She was being silly, all over some rocks.

She focused on the man. It was Reg Smith, owner of the

mercantile where she did her shopping. He was a handsome man, made to look older than he likely was by his salt-and-pepper hair. She had met him when J.B. had taken her to the store when she first arrived in town and seen him on subsequent shopping trips. He held a bundle under his arm. "How do you do, Mr. Smith? Do you have washing for me?"

"Call me Reg," he said as he handed over his bundle of washing, and then peered around the camp. "Everything O.K. here?"

She was startled anew. And then she remembered he was J.B.'s friend. "Did J.B. ask you to look in on me?" she asked as she placed his clothes in a basket.

"Well, yes. I think he'll feel better knowing that you know there's a friend nearby, just in case." His accent said he was a Yankee, which Delia found interesting, since he was J.B.'s friend yet J.B. had fought for the Confederacy. Reg casually walked over to her little path that ran up to the spring, and she could see him studying the rocks that lined the trail, and the tamped-down dirt with which she'd filled the divots last night.

Reg completed his survey and faced Delia, a small smile playing on his lips. He studied her for a moment, and she steeled herself against the questions she anticipated. She knew J.B. was concerned about her, but if she wouldn't discuss it with him, she certainly wouldn't with Reg Smith. He studied her a moment longer, and then said, "I hear you don't like the soap you bought from me."

That wasn't what she expected. She tried to relax her shoulders, even as she marveled at the gossip that traveled even in a town full of men. "Too much lye. It's terribly rough on my hands." She fluttered her hands in front of her. Reg nodded. She continued, "I'm going to make my own. I have nearly enough ashes to make my own lye, and I've been saving my cooking grease and fat for tallow. I'm going to put some pine oil in it, too, to make it smell pleasant."

Reg nodded again, and then tipped his head toward the laundry basket. "When should I return?"

After he left, Delia returned to her washing. She pushed the rocks and the memories from her mind and chose a pair of pants to scrub.

CHAPTER 16

J.B. picked his way down the trail, acting as casual as he could when he wanted to jump for joy. He'd found a small gold deposit a few weeks before; he'd wanted to tell Cal about it when he was in Gallatin City. It was enough to take care of Cal and him for a year or two, if they were frugal with their shares. Or, enough for Cal to start improving his land, and for J.B. to buy some.

But now! This past week he'd been digging like the devil. He was frustrated by how Delia had pulled away from him since that episode with the rocks dug out of the path. It clearly bothered her, though she wouldn't admit it. But she'd been avoiding him, working hard and so he had done the same.

Today, he'd uncovered a little tiny piece of ore, definitely with gold in it, but in a rock formation just like last time. He was almost certain more gold would be found. He wanted to dance with joy, but the surest way to get robbed, or worse, was let everyone know you'd struck gold.

"Evenin', Sir," said a voice to his left. He looked up to see one of his men – one of his former men, from the War. He was raggedly looking, and clearly suffering the effects of mining without success. The man tipped his hat to J.B. His respect made J.B. a little uncomfortable. He'd done what he had to do during battle. It was half luck that he'd saved his men, despite the heavy losses around them, and despite losing a portion of his own foot. He fished a tiny piece of gold from his poke bag and handed it to the man in the guise of a handshake. "You take care, you hear?" he said. The man's eyes took on a shine as he bobbed his head.

J.B. watched the man shuffle off. That man worked just as hard as J.B. but hadn't discovered the right location. It was the luck of the draw.

And J.B.'s own luck was running high. He'd come to Montana Territory to find his pot of gold so that he could make his dreams come true. If this was happening, then he'd better decide what those dreams were. Too many men, if they even discovered any gold, celebrated until they had a good idea, but the celebrations lasted longer than the funds. He wasn't going to let this happen to him.

He'd had a vague idea about getting land. There was a parcel he'd been eying, back on the other side of the hills that flanked Virginia City, right along the Madison River. Between the river and the creek that ran through it that bit of land seemed safe, even in this dry country. Maybe soon, he could claim it before someone else did. Or, he could head back over the Gallatin Valley, near Cal's homestead.

All around the mining towns there were needs for beef and other meat animals, grains and vegetables. The market was there. On the other hand, the weather in Montana Territory was harsh. Hot and dry in the summer, cold and colder in the winter. Did he want to work the land? He could see the needs for all sorts of businesses, if he wanted to try his hand at one of them.

As he continued down the path, he thought vaguely of a family. Once he saw the dearth of women out here, he'd wondered how he could manage it. He didn't have a girl back home to send for. He could ask his sisters to choose a girl for him, but knew most of their friends and couldn't see the appeal in any of them. Some fellows were sending for mail-order brides, but he would rather know her first.

And, to top it all off, he had met a gal who seemed to meet all his criteria for a wife he hadn't known he wanted. Two days before, he'd come home with an aching foot. He been carrying too much weight hauling dirt and rocks, and his bad foot suffered for it. Even the toes he didn't have seemed to ache. Delia had shoved him onto a stool alongside his cabin and dragged over a bucket of warm water.

"Now, J.B.," Delia had said, "Don't give me any guff. You need to soak that foot." He had been too tired to argue. He leaned down to slide his boot off. She'd grabbed it away.

"My goodness, this is heavy. Are you hiding gold in there?" She'd laughed at what he imagined was a look of astonishment on his face. He'd never thought to hide his gold in his boot... and he had more room in his boot than most men.

When he pulled off his sock and cotton padding, Delia had exclaimed over the red welts and blisters on his skin. He didn't have any sensation along his scars to feel the irritations and was glad they weren't worse.

Last evening, he'd returned to find Delia sitting outside, trying to catch the last of the sun's glow, knitting a new sock for him. She had a pot of stew on, hanging where her boiling pot usually hung, right out in the yard. She'd had her basket of mending next to her, and he saw his own shirt right on top with a new button sewn on.

She was beautiful, hard-working, smart, kind...and brave. No woman came to this area without some courage. She came out on her own and when her plans didn't work out, she didn't run home; she figured out a new one.

What he wondered was how much she wanted to stick to

her original plan? Did she still want Cal? How long till she admitted Cal wasn't coming to marry her? J.B. didn't know what was going on, but he sure hoped Cal would either show up and marry her or set her free. And now, he really found himself hoping for the latter. At least, that was what he was thinking he hoped. He hurried to get home to Delia.

He found her immediately. It looked like she was hanging her last basket of clothing. She pulled out a wet shirt and tossed it over the rope. She held it in place with a wooden line peg. She had her sleeves turned up to her elbows. Her apron was damp and the hair around her face was damp and curly. She looked tired, but also satisfied. She paused to look around the camp at the hanging wet laundry and the shelf he built alongside her shack, where'd she'd stacked the dried and folded clothes ready for pickup. He saw her glance at the buckets, sigh, and reach back into the basket of wet clothes.

"Delia! Aren't you finished yet?"

She raised her eyebrows in mock disapproval but kept working. "Some of us work full days. We don't stop working just because the clock says it's quitting time."

J.B. laughed. He reached into the basket and pulled out a damp shirt. He held it up to the line so that Delia could peg it into place. They continued down the line, telling jokes and stories of their day. Just as they finished, Michael Flaherty, one of Delia's customers and his friend, arrived to pick up his clean laundry, pushing a wheelbarrow.

"I've got your mail," Michael Flaherty said with his Irish lilt, reaching into his front pocket and then handing J.B. an envelope. Then he turned to Delia. "Reg told me you're going to make some sweet-smelling soap. Here's my contribution." He pointed to the wheelbarrow full of ashes with a flourish. "The finest hardwood ashes, my dear."

"Oh, Mr. Flaherty, only the finest gifts from you," Delia laughed. "Would you put them over there?" She pointed alongside her cabin to the ash hopper, where she would make lye water for her soap-making, and to the shovel. "And I'll get your clothes."

While Delia selected one stack of clothes from the many on the shelf, Michael turned to J.B.

"I just heard the news. Is this going to change things for you?"

J.B. tried to act casual, but his inner panic rose like a king tide. How could Flaherty know? He considered sprinting into his cabin to make sure his secret stash of gold nuggets and dust was still there, hidden beneath the floor in his root cellar, or sprinting back to stand guard at his claim. He pulled his attention back to the Irishman who was still talking. "I can't see you sharing that little cabin with newlyweds."

"What?" He couldn't quite process Michael's words, except he felt a welling of relief that his gold strike was still a secret. Michael slapped his leg and laughed out loud. "You're further behind than a caboose on a long train." J.B. laughed, too, because Michael's humor was so infectious. He could see that Delia was torn between desperately wanting to know what was going on and laughing.

Michael pointed to the envelope. "I think I know what's in that. You'd better open it."

J.B. glanced at the envelope in his hand. After a glance back at Michael, who was watching him with anticipation, J.B. opened the envelope and began to read. It was a note from Cal.

Dear J.B., the trouble is over…I've gotten hitched…please tell Delia how sorry I am…we will come to Virginia City soon…please help Delia until then…

He looked up to see Michael and Delia watching him. Michael waved his hand in the air, like he was plucking words from it. "Gossip travels faster than mail," he said, and added, "Grand news, I'd say."

He was answered with silence. His eyes slid from J.B. to Delia and back again.

"What is it?" Michael and Delia asked at the same time.

"Cal. He…" J.B. wondered why Cal couldn't have written a note directly to Delia. "He's gone and married that other gal."

Delia took a step back, her hand on her chest. "I…ah…"

The smile on Michael's face dropped. "I'm sorry, Ms. Delia. You mentioned a fiancé, but I didn't realize it was Cal." He floundered for a moment, and then added, "I know there's plenty of men around here who'd love to marry you, Ms. Delia…"

J.B. glared so hard that Michael's eyes widened and he stopped talking.

J.B.'s elation had surged back, but he was trying to hide it. His excitement for what this could mean for him was tempered when he saw Delia turn away toward her buckets, trying to hide disappointment in her face.

"I'm going to get some water." She grabbed two buckets and headed toward the spring.

His eyes followed her up the trail. After a moment, Michael tapped him on the shoulder. "Could this be good news for you?"

J.B. shrugged, but he allowed himself the tiniest of smiles. "I'm hoping."

CHAPTER 17

Delia mumbled something about finishing up her work and grabbed her buckets. She headed toward the spring. Though it wasn't a far walk, it would give her a moment to compose herself and figure out what this news meant for her. She stared at the clear water dribbling out of ground, caught in a half-pipe to drip out the spout over the stones.

She'd strongly suspected that Calvin was not going to come back and marry her when he got his troubles fixed, but even, so she'd had mixed feelings. A part of her, a weak, cowardly part, had wanted him to come marry her and save her from her troubles. Another, braver, part, liked being free of the burden of a false engagement. She was free to live life on her own.

But it had felt safer, here in this territory of men, being an affianced woman rather than a single one. Or, at least, acting like she was one. It didn't slow the advances of the men down much, but it helped a little. J.B. helped her because Cal asked him to. And where would she live if Calvin and his bride wanted to live in one of the cabins? J.B. would need the other.

And the final part, a small part buried deep but with a light burning so she couldn't miss it even when she tried, felt a dream spark a little brighter. Could she find a true love? Had she found the beginnings of it already?

She heard movement behind her and knew it was J.B. even before he spoke. "Are you terribly disappointed?" he asked. He was close, but not touching her. He reached down and pulled the empty buckets from her hands. He knelt to put one under the spout to catch the water and looked back at her. "Are you?"

She thought about it, wanting to give him – and herself – a truthful answer. She reached down to run her fingers under the cold splash of water. "I'm disappointed that my plans have gone so far astray that I'm left feeling unsure about my future – and even my present. But not terribly so. It had seemed to me that Calvin was truly smitten with that gal, so I'm not very surprised. But it's also freeing. I have no obligations or ties now."

Except, perhaps, I'm still married, she thought. But she didn't say it aloud.

The look J.B. gave her was questioning, and she suspected that he thought she was withholding something. She smiled brightly at J.B., not willing to elaborate. He squinted his eyes at her for a moment. Then, he looked away to move the full bucket to the side and the empty bucket under the spout.

"You could have ties if you want them."

She deliberately misunderstood him, wanting more time to think this through. She made herself laugh, "Oh, you've been taking lessons from Michael Flaherty. As if I'm going to shack up with one of the mining bums around here."

"Bums?" He stopped in his tracks.

"I didn't mean you! You're no bum. Oh, you're just funning me again." They both laughed, but it seemed forced on both sides.

Even so, she was still smiling an hour later when she finished organizing and cleaning her worksite. She knew J.B. was interested in courting her, now that Cal was out of the way, and she was considering it. Steven was dead – or gone; he would have come back by now if he'd wanted to. She hung her broom on the cabin wall hook. Everything was prepared to start fresh the next day.

Delia heard a knock. She had been sitting with her knitting in her hand, unmoving, for a while going over the events of the day. Perhaps the word was out that her fiancé had jilted her, that he'd gone and married another woman. Maybe this was Bertha, coming to renew her offer to give Delia a job in the brothel.

She put down her knitting and opened the door. J.B. stood in the doorway, silhouetted by the soft light of the moon and stars from above, and the soft glow of the lantern behind her.

"You're still up, good." He smiled. "Grab your shawl. Hurry!"

She did, wrapping it around her shoulders. She blew out her lantern and followed J.B., closing the door behind her. J.B. lightly put his hand on her back, guiding her while her eyes adjusted. He was walking with a bounce in his step and hurrying her down the street.

"What-?" she tried to ask, but he cut her off.

"You'll see, in just a minute."

They were headed downtown, and ahead Delia saw the light of torches. Growing louder were the sounds of men's voices, which broke out into Irish shanty songs. They turned a corner and J.B. led her onto a boardwalk. Standing behind a hitching post, they had a good view of the parade.

And that's what it was. An impromptu parade. Dozens of men, many looking fairly inebriated, were marching down the road. They carried torches and mugs of beer, and in the middle, one man was carried on the shoulders of others. He was smiling and reaching out, shaking hands as the mass undulated down the road.

"Who's that?" Delia asked.

"Thomas Meagher. He's just arrived in town. He's the new territorial secretary; the second in command after the governor."

Delia couldn't help but smile at the rowdy welcome the secretary was receiving. She looked down the road a bit and saw Big Bertha standing on her own boardwalk. She was a beacon of rose-colored femininity lit by the torches. She was waving at the men in the parade who gave her a 'huzzah!' "The union general?" she asked, glancing at J.B.

"The same. But I don't think it's his war status that gained him this attention in such a Southern-built town as Virginia City. I'd say it's an Irish welcome for an Irish hero."

Delia felt a snag on her skirt. She looked down to see Chatty's little dog pawing at her.

"Oh, you!" She reached out a foot to gently push the dog off her skirt. "You're going to rip my skirt. Shoo."

The dog continued to nose around her. "It's that soap, isn't? I never met a dog that wanted to eat soap as much as you do. You're going to get sick." J.B. reached down and picked up the dog. He held it in front of Delia for a moment. "No," she said in a silly voice, "I don't carry soap around for dogs." J.B. dropped the dog down on the road and the noise and excitement even caught up the dog, so that it continued down the street with the parade.

Delia and J.B. continued to watch the parade slowly making its way down the street, until the group had mostly passed. With the torches gone, and only a few lights shining out the windows, the street was shadowed and they were reminded of the coolness of the night. Nearby murmurs were heard. Delia and J.B. walked back to the cabins in quiet conversation. They didn't discuss Cal or his recent marriage.

CHAPTER 18

J.B. was barely awake when he heard a pounding. He could see through the cracks in the shutters that the sky was just turning pink. The birds were chirping happily, but the pounding knocks did not sound happy. He called out, "Hang on." He pulled on his pants, shirt, and boots. If they weren't shouting too, he figured his roof wasn't on fire.

He pulled open the door to find Michael Flaherty standing there.

"Sorry to wake you, J.B. I was getting an early start and looking to your back yard on my way by." He pointed over J.B.'s shoulder toward the yard and Delia's home, as though J.B.'s cabin was not in the way. J.B.'s brows lowered.

"Can't blame me for trying to catch glimpse of the prettiest lass in Virginia City," said Michael with a little shrug. "Anyway, someone's been making mischief back there."

They hurried around the building and J.B. stopped short when he saw the yard.

All the clotheslines were down, and all of the clothes that Delia had washed and hung to dry lay in heaps on the ground. His first thought was a buck elk or deer careening through camp, catching the ropes with its antlers. But he knew no animal would have dropped all the lines, all still in neat rows. He walked over to check out the ends of the ropes, but even before he got close, he could see the knots that he'd nailed to the walls were still there with short but clean-cut stubs of rope left. Someone had cut the lines.

J.B. turned back to Michael. "Did you see anyone?"

Michael shook his head.

"I don't get it. Who'd want to harm a pretty lass who does the wash?"

J.B. shrugged. "Thanks for waking me. I'll go wake Delia."

Michael headed back down the path past J.B.'s cabin.

First, J.B. walked around the yard, looking for any clues as to who did this. He couldn't see any boot prints that stood out. There were lots of men coming and going every day, to drop off and pick up laundry. He'd seen them assaying Delia when she wasn't looking. A few of the bold ones did it when she was looking. He'd even seen that greasy Freddy out along the road here a little too often.

The ropes had been cut by a knife, but everyone carried one. The only thing he saw to note was that another rock had been dug up and put to the side of the walking area, this one near the door to the shack. He didn't like seeing that anyone had been so close to the door to Delia in the night. He gave a bang on the door and then didn't wait. He tried to open the door but realized she had barred it.

He shouted as he banged again on the door. "Delia! Are you alright in there?"

"J.B.? Is that you? Hold on, I'll be right there." After a long moment, she opened the door in her nightdress. She was wrapping a shawl wrapped around her shoulders and her hair was in a plait which hung over her shoulder down to her elbow. She rubbed her eyes and tried to stifle a yawn. "What's the matter?"

"I'm glad you're safe." Relief flooded through him…and something else. Her natural beauty struck him and for a moment he couldn't remember why he was at her door so early. She looked inquiringly at him, and he knew she trusted him not to wake her for no good reason. "I'm sorry to be the bearer of bad news. Someone vandalized your laundry."

That woke her up. She quickly stepped past him to see the cut lines and clothes crumpled on the ground. "Oh!" She let out a gasp and brought her hands to her mouth.

After a moment, she started looking in every direction, as though the perpetrator would be standing by, waiting to be caught out. "There's no one about, Delia. I've looked around."

"I…I've got to get dressed." She turned to go back inside, her shoulders hunched and her hands gripping the shawl like she was very cold. She stopped when she saw a stone that had been pried out of the packed dirt yard and left next to its former home, staring at it silently.

J.B.'s hands automatically started reaching out to comfort Delia, but she stepped away. It wasn't his place, it seemed.

"I'm going to go get help. I'll be back soon."

He wanted to comfort her, or see her flamed up with anger, but her silence was discomfiting.

CHAPTER 19

It took Delia three tries to lace up her shoes. She kept tangling the laces and missing hooks. Every rustle, crackle, and knock had her on edge. She was scared.

She'd been through this before. The rocks. Bad things happening. It would only get worse.

She had nowhere else to run. No ideas, little money.

Her hands shook as she reached behind her back to tie her apron. One step at a time. She carefully opened the door and looked around. No one.

She found an empty tub and set it on the ground. One by one, she unpinned each item of clothing, placing the clothespin into her pocket, shook it out, and inspected it for dirt or tears. The clothes were dry and seemed to have dropped down with little extra movement. Some shirts she could brush off, fold and put in her finished stacks. Some had smudges and streaks that meant she would have to wash them again. Those, she tossed into the tub. Nothing so far had rips or tears that hadn't been there already. Her ash hopper had not been tipped over, for which she was grateful. What a mess that would have been.

She had just finished the first row when J.B. returned with

Reg Smith. She didn't stop to greet them but simply gave them a nod. Reg started walking the yard, staring at the ground. He fingered the ropes and checked her shelves and tubs. She hadn't even thought to inspect what didn't appear damaged.

J.B. stood by her side, also watching Reg. He moved close, a hovering guardian angel. She stepped farther, in the guise of wrapping up the cut rope. He reached out to take it from her. As though oblivious, she laid the ring of rope on the edge of the fire pit. She could tell he wanted to help her, but it was best to keep her distance.

"He runs the mercantile. Why is he here?" she asked, gesturing to Reg.

"He used to be a lawman. Doesn't advertise it, given the behavior of our recent lawmen," said J.B., referring to the local sheriff who'd been hanged the year before for running a gang of road agents. J.B. hung his thumbs in his belt, as if daring her to challenge him.

The storeowner joined them. "I was a deputy sheriff back before the war, in New England, and then did some intelligence work during it. I've had enough of that, but you can't unlearn what you know." He turned with his palm uplifted, like he had a platter with evidence on it. Or not. "Nothing here that'll tell us who did this."

Now he turned his intense eyes on Delia. "Do you have any ideas?"

She didn't want to lie, but she didn't want to tell the truth, either. That could backfire, especially if this man was used to upholding the law. And J.B., he might not want her to stay either.

She looked back at Reg. "No. No idea." No idea how to get out of this mess.

It was J.B.'s turn. "Delia, have any of your customers been giving you trouble? Hanging around?"

This she could answer truthfully. "No, no trouble. I've seen that Freddy hanging around a few times. He makes my skin crawl, but he keeps his distance."

Just then, a man walked into the yard. He was one of her customers, but looking straight at J.B. "You need help, sir? I see you had some trouble. After all you done for me in the War, it's the least I can do."

Delia wanted to feel grateful, but she resented how this man went to J.B. It was her laundry. Her life. Things were turning bad. Again. It started with the rocks, and then vandalism. How long until someone got hurt?

She turned away and started collecting the clothes from the next row. She needed more rope. She needed a big knife.

CHAPTER 20

Delia wouldn't take his help cleaning up. The more J.B. tried, the more agitated she became. She didn't want his help picking up the clothes. She didn't want him stoking the fire for the new wash she'd have to do. He was just returning with buckets full of water when she turned to him abruptly and said, "Just go."

"Don't shoot the messenger."

She glared at him.

But instead of J.B., it was Delia who left, gone to walk to the mercantile to buy more rope. The shop routinely ran out of flour and other basics, but rope was in good supply, usually. J.B. hadn't liked her walking alone, but she'd glared at him something fierce, and said, "I'm perfectly safe."

For the life of him, the more he studied mining, the more success he had discovering gold. But the more he studied the fairer sex, the less success he had. Pretty soon, he wouldn't know a damn thing about women.

Since she wasn't here to say no, J.B. tied a few of the shorter ropes together and then hung them from the nails in the exterior walls. Delia might not like his help when she returned, but she was going to need someone's help and he'd rather it be his.

One thing J.B. knew from his time in the mining camp was that this turn of events wasn't good. Mining didn't discriminate; both good and bad men were attracted to the promise of something better. The war had turned good men bad and bad men into something that wasn't even human.

He hadn't seen anyone acting troublesome. Nor had he heard of any other vandals in the area. There was thievery, brawling, drunkenness, even murder, but most men didn't destroy things for no reason. This was personal. It was about Delia. J.B. didn't know what was worse: a total unknown character, watching and harassing Delia; or one of the men he did know, acting friendly and fine while plotting terrible things. The thing that bothered him the most...Delia was upset, angry, even confused...but not shocked. Not surprised enough.

J.B. thought of how they'd walked home in the near dark. He'd left Delia at her door, waiting until she'd lit her lantern and barred the door. He had walked across the yard to his cabin, so lost in thought he hadn't looked around at all. He was certain the lines were still hung then; he'd have noticed if they were down. But was the culprit there, watching them in the dark? Had he walked right by the vandal? Had Delia?

CHAPTER 21

J.B. was hovering again. Delia could sense him behind her, two benches back, wanting to ensure her safety even though she was perfectly safe at a church service. She'd come here for comfort, as always, but hadn't found as much as she'd hoped for. Today was no different. It was hard to accept the friendship of others, or even God's grace, when you felt like a fraud.

The church women, among the few in town not affiliated with Big Bertha, had been welcoming to Delia. But she was presenting herself as a jilted fiancée—when that had been a tenuous hope at best since before she'd arrived in Virginia City —and as a widow, also a questionable role.

Word of her cut laundry lines had spread quickly. It was four days since the incident and Delia was tired of saying, "No, I have no idea who did this!" and "I'm afraid someone too far gone with drink just wasn't thinking clearly." She felt rather stupid saying it, in fact, but couldn't bear to discuss it over and over.

As the hymn ended, Delia glanced over her shoulder. J.B. was looking right at her with a questioning, hesitant expression.

Hesitant, because she had snapped at him yesterday and the day before, and the day before that. Every day since the incident, in fact. He prowled the camp every morning and every evening, looking for clues of a trespasser. He prowled the neighborhood, looking for strangers. Since new men were pouring in on a near daily basis, Delia wasn't sure how fruitful that activity was.

He meant well, and that was why she felt bad for what she was about to do. If she couldn't get him to back off, she was going to have to leave. Her staying only put his life in danger.

Back in Missouri, folks had been kind to her when Steven went missing in action. She hadn't known if he had been captured by the enemy, killed, or was in a hospital, injured and unable to identify himself. She hadn't been sure which predicament she was hoping for.

But she had wondered. Steven had come to town, nephew of a local shopkeeper. He'd said he was looking for new opportunities, and since his uncle had no offspring of his own, this made sense to everyone. Not long after he'd arrived, his aunt had passed away. The two men, the younger and the older, had been as close as bark to the tree. It was Uncle Geoffrey who had encouraged his nephew to settle down and start his own family.

Steven had been handsome and charming, and swept her off her feet. He'd changed very quickly after they'd married. He was sweet at times, and angry at others. She learned he'd left his home for other reasons, darker reasons. She learned it was very difficult to be married to a man whose behavior changed with the wind.

Delia remembered how he insisted on the most precise housekeeping. His handkerchiefs had to be folded and ironed in perfect quarters. The dishes needed to be stacked precisely on the shelf. Plates on the left, bowls on the right. The mugs, hung underneath the shelf on their little hooks, all had to face the same direction. She was to wear a crisp, clean apron at all times; she'd become an expert at tying a perfect bow behind her back.

Her relief when her husband had left to go to war was palpable. At last, she no longer had to walk on eggshells. One day, for no other reason than that she could, she rearranged the plates and bowls. She hung the mugs in different directions. She ripped off her apron and tossed it over the back of a chair. She wore a dress she hadn't ironed. Who would see it? Who would care? She felt a lightness in her heart that she hadn't felt since she moved out of her parents' house.

And there she was, leaning over a mixing bowl with cookie dough – with extra sugar and cinnamon as she liked it and as Steven never did – when her husband's uncle arrived.

"Delia." He always did that; said her name thunderously and waited until she stopped what she was doing and gave him her full attention. "You are denigrating your marriage. You have an obligation to your husband. To obey him."

She'd been so startled that she actually looked around the kitchen for Steven. "He's not here."

"But." There was that thunder again. "You know his wishes. Do you think they don't count because he's not here? Because he's off at war? What if he were to walk through that door this instant?" He waited, glaring at her, until she picked up her apron. She tied it on, with its perfect bow. He waited until she walked over to the shelves, until the plates and bowls and mugs were all arranged. She tried not to look at the bowl of cookie dough, afraid that Geoffrey would somehow notice the extra sugar already mixed in and chastise her for waste-fulness.

And then. Then, he had smiled, his tense posture relaxing. He'd walked over to her and placed his hands on her shoul-ders, heavy. He'd stared into her eyes. "You are lucky to be married to our Steven. He is a fine, upstanding young man. If

I'd had my own son, I could not have hoped for more." He'd gone on in that vein for a while. He was, effectively, her father-in-law. And, in Steven's absence, she was dependent on him for so much. She had stood there and listened.

She heard about this day again, in a letter from Steven. Her husband's letters were all that a new husband's letters should be, except that each contained a response to a report from his uncle. *You mustn't spend so much time engaging the pastor's wife after Church. You should not have spent so much on your new dress. You are not maintaining the garden properly.* Worst of all, Steven feared she'd take up with another man, and her uncle's reports did nothing to diminish the fear. *I hear you are flirting with Ian MacDonald. I told you I didn't want you to hire that Scotsman. Get rid of him. Or, there may be an accident.*

She wrote back, trying to reassure him, but his threat had shocked her. She let Ian go. She read the casualty lists in the newspapers and tried very hard not to admit she was perhaps hoping to see his name. She felt a terrible guilt.

After he'd been missing for two months, she felt certain he had perished, and been buried in a mass grave with so many other soldiers. Her husband's uncle had refused to consider this. He would not allow her to hold a service, or wear widow's weeds. The neighbors prodded her gently, considering her a naïve but loving wife who was too hopeful. Mrs. Albertson sent her second oldest son to help her. Jimmy, only seventeen, would stop by a few times a week to chop wood, do repairs, or what-not. She would laugh with the boy and his friendly smile gave her something to look forward to. There was no romance, but a friendship between two young people. Even so, Geoffrey had glowered when he stopped by, telling her Steven wouldn't approve.

And then one day, when she was in town shopping, she had a visitor. Someone chopped her a big stack of wood. No one admitted to being her helper, but they stacked it like Steven used to do, in precise formation. It was, she thought, a coincidence. Then there were stones upturned from her paths, along the road she walked, around the house. Just like Steven used to do.

It was soon after this that she received a note from Mrs. Albertson, delivered by the youngest son. Jimmy had been in an accident and had two broken legs. She could not spare another son at this time. The boy told her that Jimmy had been thrown from his horse, that his girdle had broken. It was an unusual accident, and made her think of Steven's threat about the hired man.

Could Steven be back? This did not make any sense. But it was enough for Delia to write to Steven's commanding officer, asking if there was any news. There wasn't. Her husband was missing after a battle. Some men had gone running, cowards, and officially they couldn't be sure Steven wasn't one of them. This officer felt certain Steven was dead, but it wasn't official with no body or anyone who had seen his death.

So, she was alone, close to penniless. Unable to hire help. Afraid to accept the kindness of her neighbors, for their own safety. She could not even don widow's weeds and seek a new husband in town. She didn't like Steven's uncle and didn't want to be reliant on him, forced to pretend she was waiting for her husband to return.

That was why she had agreed to come out West. She would claim her widowhood, but also a new husband, and start over. It hadn't worked exactly as she'd planned, but it had seemed to be working. Until these recent events.

Steven was dead.

But what if he wasn't?

But if he wasn't, why didn't he come back to her? In Missouri or here?

If Steven wasn't dead and had followed her here,

maybe…maybe it didn't matter. She couldn't let J.B. get hurt. His hovering, his attention – she had to stop it.

She left church. She smiled and nodded to others, but all along she was aware of J.B. hovering nearby. She waited until they were away from the other churchgoers, halfway home, before she turned to him.

"Must you follow me everywhere?" she said through gritted teeth.

A look of surprise and hurt flashed across his face. "I came to ask if you'd seen anyone in church that was making you uncomfortable?"

"No! You've asked me every day, and the answer is no! Not at home. Not at the store. Not at church." Her low, angry voice cut between them. "The prankster is gone and only you won't let it go. You go back to your mine and leave me to my work. You're protecting me from nothing and just won't leave me in peace."

J.B.'s eyebrows drew. His voice was low and intense. "You don't fool me. I see how easily you startle. I see you looking around, always looking around. I see how you walk wider turns around corners, so that someone lurking there can't surprise you. I see the knife you have in your apron pocket."

This startled her. She knew he'd been looking around, but she hadn't known he'd been looking at her. He held his hand out, a gesture of peacemaking. "Look, Delia—"

She cut him off.

"Must I leave? I found it convenient to work and live here, but if this doesn't work for you—"

"What? No, I didn't mean —"

"I don't know what you meant, but I can't live like this." Her voice caught, for this was true, and she felt it deep inside. "I am not yours to protect, and I don't want your protection. I want you to be my landlord, and nothing more. Nothing." She didn't know how she could start over again. How could she survive if Steven were still following her, doing this again and again? But nor could she allow J.B., sweet kind J.B., to be hurt.

She didn't know if J.B. was reacting to her anger, or her desperation, but he dropped his hand and stepped back. He gave a quick shake of his head, like he was shaking off a shade that had been clouding his vision. "Fine. Just make sure my property doesn't get damaged by your pranksters." He twirled around and stalked away.

She knew he was angry, and maybe hurt, by seeing the way he walked. His limp was always more pronounced when his emotions ran high.

Delia stood in the middle of the dusty street. In one direction was the creek, all torn up, with piles of slag lining it. In another were yet more new buildings, still smelling of fresh-cut wood. It seemed everyone in Virginia City was overturning their past and starting afresh. She took a deep breath. She would do it, too.

Again.

She looked around for another moment. She had better start keeping an eye out for a new location. Or a new town. J.B. would not give up so easily.

CHAPTER 22

J.B. feigned anger, and then indifference. He stomped around for a day, stopped circling the wagons, and focused on his mine again. The anger wasn't hard. He was angry at how Delia had treated him. Here he was, mooning over her and dreaming of a future together, and she was treating him like a stray dog at the kitchen door. But he was angered more by the fact that she felt she had to do this. He wasn't a vain man, so when his instincts had told him she cared, he believed them.

But she clearly felt she had to protect him, and this was her way of doing so. Someone was still watching her. At least, she thought so. And so did he.

Did she think he couldn't protect her, because of his foot? He was busting his hump every day at the mine, but maybe that wasn't enough for her. Maybe this was just an excuse to push him away. After the news of Cal's marriage J.B. was ready to court Delia. She might need time to adjust her thinking, but he didn't really think she was heartbroken over Cal. Maybe J.B. simply wasn't enough of a man for her.

In war, sometimes you were the predator, and sometimes

the prey. At this moment, J.B. could sense a predator, feeling the hairs on the back of his neck rise up suddenly. It wasn't what he could see that had him nervous; it was what he couldn't. He really didn't want this responsibility again, but he couldn't not help. Especially since it was Delia.

So, very quietly, he recruited a few fellows to help keep an eye on her when he wasn't there. Reg, Michael, Chatty, and even Big Bertha's boy Kit, whom everyone overlooked. Plus, there were a few soldiers from Wilson's Creek who felt they owed J.B., because they hadn't become one of the many casualties of that battle. He didn't feel they owed him, but maybe this could make it even in their minds. He had even taken his hand drill one night in the dark, to make a tiny eye-hole in the back of his cabin. He could slide a hanging pot aside and see down the path to the creek. He felt a bit like a peeping Tom, but he would do anything, he realized, to keep Delia safe.

So, J.B. headed to the mine. He followed Alder Creek, all rock and destruction, to a smaller creek. Right off of Alder, this one was also torn up, but having revealed little to interest the miners, the creek quickly morphed into its natural state. He was about to head off onto another trail that led to his claim when a movement in the brush caught his eye.

In the red willow brush along the creek was a young moose calf. Already close to five feet tall, it had frozen with a mouthful of leaves. It was, he thought, a beautiful young animal, standing next to the stream sparkling with the morning light. Even as he thought this, he caught the movement of a full-grown mama moose. She snorted and charged him. It didn't matter that she didn't have antlers; she looked like she weighed 600 pounds.

J.B. leapt to the side, but still got knocked by the moose's shoulder, standing at the same height as his own. He scrambled to his feet and raced toward a cottonwood tree. Just as his hand touched the deeply grooved wood, he caught his good foot under a root and felt the ankle twist. He managed to wrap his arm around the trunk enough to keep from falling over and scramble around it. The moose charged by the tree and turned around. He shuffled around, and by doing this several times, always keeping the tree between himself and the moose, he managed to outlast the protective aggression of the mother moose.

When she finally walked away, J.B. rested his head on the bark of the old cottonwood tree. It was clearly rotten and failing, and that was the only reason someone hadn't cut it down for lumber.

The cow moose grunted to her calf. Together, they crossed the creek and disappeared in the willow wetlands. He stayed at the tree, watching to make sure she left the vicinity, for ten whole minutes. In that time, his ankle began to throb, and by the feeling in his boot, swell.

Trying to walk back up the trail was excruciating. To keep as much weight off his injured foot as possible, he had to use his partial foot. Even with his special boot, the scar tissue and nerve damage made the extra weight-bearing painful. Several times he had pain shooting out of one foot or the other, twice bad enough that he reeled and lost his balance, falling down again.

A man on the frontier with two bad feet, a mine unsecured, a partner out of town, a lone woman on the defensive...and today, he didn't feel good about life.

The first person J.B. saw when he got back into town was Freddy. He was coming out of a shadowy alley, some other fellow heading deeper into the gloom. *Some people are always causing trouble,* J.B. thought. Freddy smirked at the limping J.B., but he didn't say a word.

At the next corner, he ran into Reg. "Shouldn't you be behind your counter?" J.B. asked, striving for levity. Reg grabbed J.B.'s arm and slung it over his shoulder. "Shouldn't you be in a hospital?"

He squeezed his eyes shut for a moment, holding his breath in pain. He gasped, "Funny thing, there doesn't seem to be one around here."

Reg acted as a crutch, helping J.B. all the way home. He promised to stop by Big Bertha's on his way back to the mercantile and have her send Kit to find the doctor.

J.B. was looking forward to collapsing on his bed. His collar and hands were sweat-dampened. He tried to distract himself as they approached the camp, imagining Delia running to him when she caught sight of him. Maybe she'd cry out, "Oh, J.B. You're hurt!'"

Instead, as J.B. and Reg limped into sight, she looked up and froze. After a brief moment, she put down the bucket she was carrying from the spring and headed down the path toward them. "I guess I'm going to have to help you." His heart sank.

She slowly walked over, put his other arm over her shoulder, and along with Reg, helped drag J.B. into his cabin.

CHAPTER 23

Delia was having a hard time appearing heartless. She'd seen the disappointment in J.B.'s eyes, and the disapproval in Reg's, when she'd spoken so callously. But seeing J.B. injured, his face white with pain, this was her greatest fear. She'd nearly run to him but forced herself to hold still until she had herself under control. The only way to keep things from getting worse was to act as though she didn't care.

"Don't cut my boot off!" he squawked from the bed. She stood there with a big pair of shears in her hands.

"It has to come off."

"Where the heck am I going to get new boots around here? And I'd have to rebuild my custom boot if I want one to match." He was lying on his back with one arm thrown over his face. She saw one eye peeking out, focused on the shears.

She lay it on a table and put her hands on her hips. "I'll try to pull it off."

She pulled it off, with some effort. The pale skin of his leg that rarely saw the light of day, swollen and red around the ankle and so different from the darker weathered skin of his face…made him seem more vulnerable. He was damp with sweat when she turned around.

"Oh, J.B.," she said, pulling his handkerchief from his pocket and blotting his face. He grabbed her wrist and looked into her eyes. "You confuse me."

Tears welled in her eyes. She looked out the window, trying to regain her composure, and saw Kit leading a strange man with a black bag approaching the cabin. It was likely the doctor. She couldn't afford to be seen crying over J.B. He couldn't afford for her to do so.

She took his hand from her wrist, placed it back on his chest, and said, "Let's get the other boot off."

Later, when Kit came and asked if she needed any help, she sent for ice. Delia realized she'd been inside with J.B. for a long time…too long. J.B. looked like he wanted to sleep, but she still needed to talk to him.

"How did you twist your ankle?" That was, she thought, a perfectly reasonable question.

"I fell over a tree root." He wasn't going to elaborate, she realized after a moment.

"What were you doing?"

"Running away."

She let out a gasp and knelt at his side. Her hands were grasping his arm before she realized it. He looked at her with surprise.

"From whom?"

He eyed her carefully. "What makes you so sure it's a who?"

She was so sure it was Steven, that the question didn't even make sense to her for a moment. Of course, she was sure! And then his question sank in.

"You wouldn't run away from much, as far as I can see." She sat back on her heels and released his arm. He seemed to be testing her, without saying all that much. She didn't like it.

"That's so. I would run away from an angry cow, however."

"A wild cow?" She couldn't imagine a wild cow chasing J.B.

"Not a wild cow. A cow moose! It was a mama moose, protecting her calf. I stumbled upon them while walking the path to my mine." He filled her in on the details, even making her laugh once.

She was on her knees, facing him, while he lay back with his head turned to her at the side of the bed. They looked at each other, and Delia wondered what he was thinking. She was thinking how handsome he was, even with the strain of pain in his face. His brown eyes…

There was a knock at the door. Delia jumped up and ran to the door. It was Kit. "I been around town. There's no ice to be had. He's gonna half to soak his foot in the crick water." She nodded. He added, "Sorry Ma'am," before leaving.

Delia took a moment to look out over the town. It wasn't even midday, for all the excitement already past. The sun still shone and the laundry was still waiting for her. She walked back to J.B.'s side.

"I've got to get back to work, J.B."

"I know," he said. He looked at her with tired eyes. "I know you've been thinking of moving on."

She jerked her head up in surprise. She'd been thinking seriously about it. She neither agreed nor disagreed, though, and waited to see what J.B. wanted to say.

"I need you to wait, if you can. If you will. I need help, at least for a bit." He sounded humble, but with some pride creeping in.

Delia wanted to hug him and shake him at the same time. She wanted desperately to help him, to comfort him, to care for him. She desperately feared, though, such attention could put him in danger, that leaving him high and dry was the lesser of two evils.

"Surely, you can hire a boy, like Kit?"

"I need someone I can trust. I need you…" he tapered off, and Delia could only stare, feeling so much was being said in that need. "Please."

And she realized she couldn't leave him like this. She didn't even want to do so. She reached out, gently squeezing his hand. "I will not act happy about this. Out there." She pointed back toward the door. She didn't know if he understood what she meant, didn't want to explain, but felt he should know what to expect.

"I understand," he said soberly. He squeezed her hand back, and then pulled his hand away. He turned his head and closed his eyes.

Well, thought Delia to herself, *now we'll really see how good an actress I can be.* She walked over to the front door, wrenched it open, and stomped outside, slamming it behind her. She stomped around the cabin and right over to her laundry, left sitting in sopping heaps for the past hour and a half, mumbling to herself about burdens and delays. She didn't know if she had an audience, but wasn't taking any chances.

She stuck a couple of pieces of wood in the fire, to get the water heated up again. She grabbed a shirt and her washboard but couldn't find the soap. She looked around the tubs, on her work shelf and worktable. And then she heard that gnawing sound again. She darted around the corner of the cabin. There was that dog again! Eating her soap! "Give me that!" she cried out. The dog dropped the bar as she approached and she snatched it up. "Go on! Shoo!" she shouted at the dog. He snuck off, tail between his legs.

It was only soap, but Delia started to cry.

CHAPTER 24

J.B. sat in a chair behind his cabin, placed to allow him to see into Delia's laundry yard and the path down to the road. As he had done every day for a week, he propped his sprained ankle up on a bench. Sometimes he soaked his foot in a tub of cold water brought from the spring by Delia. Sometimes he sharpened his tools, or oiled his leathers, or carved some wood pieces. At this point, it didn't matter what he was doing. He was as fidgety as boy in church.

His attention was drawn to Delia, as always. He couldn't see her face because of the big floppy bonnet she wore, but he'd become expert at reading her body. When she felt obligated to speak to him, she was brusque, intolerant, and he replied in kind. To the world, they could barely tolerate speaking to each other. Her aid to him and his to her was merely the work of expedience, of people who needed each other even if they wished it were otherwise. Out here, in the Territories, this was not uncommon, especially for the injured and the female.

He had decided, that first day he sat outside, that if he must be trapped by his injury, he would use this time to figure out what was going on in Delia's head. And, if he was lucky, return to her good graces. And, if he was really lucky, charm her.

First, he figured out that when he wore his biggest brimmed hat, and tilted his head down, he could speak to Delia in a low voice that wasn't obvious to anyone who wasn't right nearby. And so, she wouldn't shush him; she'd listen. J.B. tried to lead her on by asking questions, but she mostly remained silent, at first. So, instead, he offered stories of himself.

"So that's why I was in Gallatin City, looking for Cal. We hit a small vein in the mine and I could pay him back. Now, anything else I find will be divided equally, my share my own, free and clear."

One day, Michael Flaherty stopped by for a visit and commented on her red nose. That was enough for Delia to bring out her own hat, a big floppy bonnet. Not long after, J.B. was surprised when a whisper of a voice reached his ear. He looked up, but Delia was head down, scrubbing a piece of clothing along the washboard. With her bonnet on, he couldn't see her lips move or her face at all, so he wasn't even sure she'd spoken to him. At first, he was annoyed. Then he heard the question softly repeated, "How did you meet Calvin?"

And then he realized Delia didn't want anyone watching to think they were talking. He was glad he had felt annoyed, and let his scowl fully develop as he looked around the area. He eyed the washtubs and the flapping clothes, and even Delia. He hoped anyone watching would think he disliked the whole business cluttering up his yard. Not that anyone in this popup town considered their yards showplaces, but a lot of fellows came out West to avoid their women-folk, or at least enjoyed a break from the proprieties that so often accompanied them.

J.B. lowered his head, looking carefully at the piece of

wood he was carving in his hand. He used his knife to whittle a piece off. "I met him out here last winter."

He turned the wood and eyed it, trying to decide where to run his knife next. He listened to the sloshing of the tub water and the slap of the cloth.

"Why did he invest with you? A stranger."

He listened beyond the sounds of the laundry but heard nothing to indicate anyone was approaching. "I helped him out of a bind. He said he had a good instinct for people and trusted me right off the bat. I said I had a mine staked out, he offered money for equipment and expenses. "

He paused but heard nothing new from Delia, so he continued. "He helps when he's in town, every month to six weeks." Or, he did, thought J.B., wondering how Cal's recent marriage would change things.

He snuck a glance. Delia was hanging a pair of long johns on the line, squeezing out extra water along the arms and legs. Her apron was damp, her sleeves rolled back showing her suntanned arms. He could see from the darkened fabric around her neck and the glisten along her skin that she was too hot. He imagined her damp hair curling around her rosy face and wished the bonnet didn't block his view.

"Out here, there isn't a lot of time to get to know a man's character. It's not like back East, where so many people grow up together, or move to town with relatives to vouch for them. You have to decide fairly quick, or else you can't trust anyone." He wondered if she was still thinking about Cal, and about not being able to marry him. Was she heartbroken and just hiding it?

He leaned down to place the knife on the ground beside his chair. He grabbed his file, ready to start smoothing the wood.

Delia returned to her rinse tub. "Is that why you were so quick to accept me?" she asked. J.B. almost didn't hear her, the words muffled by the slosh of the water as she stirred the clothes around to rinse the soap out. "Because of Cal?"

"I suppose so." He ran the file back and forth, smoothing the wood. "You had history with Cal. And you seemed respectable." He decided to take a leap. "Plus, you're awfully pretty."

He heard a snort and was tempted to laugh himself but was interrupted.

"Halloo! J.B., sir." It was another of his men from the war. The man took his hat off and nodded to J.B. as he walked up the path alongside the cabin. "I'm sorry to bother you when you're laid up, but I could use your help."

"Anything, Jessup, to save me from dying of boredom," J.B. replied, flinging his arms wide open.

"I brought you this venison haunch, sir," the man said. "I don't want you to feel obligated to assist me. You've already done so much..." Jessup's voice trailed off. Something about saving a man's life; they ended up beholden to each other, it seemed to J.B.

J.B. saw Delia pause, her stirring stick slow for just a moment.

"Jessup, you didn't need to bring me anything, but I won't say no to some fresh game. Thank you kindly." Jessup stood there, holding the wrapped haunch, waiting for J.B. to tell him what to do with it. Before J.B. could move, Delia swept in and took it. Without inflection she said, "I'll put it in your cabin." She disappeared inside, and J.B. heard her slide back the trap door to the cold storage under the floor. Then she reappeared and returned to her laundry. She never looked at J.B.

Jessup watched Delia, bemused.

"What can I do for you, Jessup?"

"Well, see, here's my dilemma. I have a claim that's showing promise." He glanced around as he said this.

J.B. responded in a similar low voice. "That's a good kind of dilemma."

Jessup flashed a smile, but a sad one. "It is. But I can't stay. My wife and children back home need me. I wish I could stay longer, but with winter coming on, I got to go." He took a deep breath. "See, I've got a fellow willing to buy my claim, but at rock bottom price. Says the ore ain't got but a speck of gold."

J.B. nodded, but didn't say anything.

Jessup continued. "I got a couple of pieces here. Would you look at them, tell me what you think?" He pulled two rocks out of his pocket. J.B. held out his hand. He turned the pieces, eyeing them from different angles. He hefted them, feeling their weight.

"I can do you better than that. Step into my cabin there, and right on that first shelf is a jar of quicksilver. Get that for me, and the pan hanging just below it." While Jessup got the supplies, J.B. got up and hobbled over to Delia. "Can we use a bit of your fire, there?"

She looked up. Her bonnet framed her face. Her green eyes shone. She gave him a quick smile and only he could see it. "You may," she said.

J.B. hobbled back to get his chair and brought it next to the fire. Jessup brought the pan and the quicksilver. J.B. placed Jessup's ore rocks in the pan and then poured quicksilver over them. He hung the pan over the fire and the ingredients started heating up.

J.B. looked up at Jessup. "Now, we wait."

Jessup leaned back on his heals and studied the mixture. They were silent.

"It's looking pretty good, ain't it?" Jessup asked.

J.B. realized he was sitting there, staring at the amalgam in the pan with a smile playing on his lips. He focused on the pan.

The quicksilver had done its job. The gold had separated from the rest of the ore, binding with the quicksilver. J.B.

waved the fumes away as he peered into the pan. It was a good amount.

"Jessup, we can't know for sure how much gold is in your claim. But I'd say you don't need to accept a rock bottom price."

Jessup had a smile that stretched from ear to ear. He grabbed J.B.'s hand and started pumping it. "Thank you, sir! Thank you. Thank you." His eyes glistened with relief.

J.B. looked over at Delia. She had paused in her work and was watching them. She didn't say a word. She barely smiled in the shadows of her bonnet. She gave him only the slightest nod. But, somehow, J.B. felt himself puff with pride.

J.B. took the pan off the fire. Jessup, mesmerized by the pan even as it cooled, didn't take his eyes off it. All his hopes rested in it.

J.B.'s eyes, on the other hand, kept turning to Delia.

CHAPTER 25

Delia eyed her red chapped hands. Her laundry business was a success, keeping her busy. But she'd never had to wash clothes six days a week before. The soap was taking a toll on her skin. It simply had too much lye in it.

Today was a rare break from the laundry, but she was still plenty busy. Today she was making her – hopefully better – soap.

Delia leaned over her pot, breathing in through the handful of sagebrush she held. The bite of the lye was still noticeable, but not as much. Unfortunately, the sagebrush had its own spicy bite and Delia wasn't sure it was an improvement. She sighed. It would be lovely to scent her lye soap with lavender, but there wasn't any available. She'd have to keep exploring the local flora to find something suitable. Until then, she'd use the pine oil she'd extracted from the branches she'd been given and hope it worked well within the soap.

"Mrs. Watson, whatever are you up to now?" It was Big Bertha, sashaying into the yard in a green velvet dress. She eyed the cauldron. As the smell of the lye wafted up, her eyes watered and she moved upwind away from the fumes.

"I'm making soap."

Big Bertha sniffed again and took a step back. She had her smooth-looking hand – not at all red and chapped – resting on her chest as though she'd been exposed to something mildly offensive. She turned to J.B., who was standing alongside his cabin, with a broom in his hand.

"J.B., are you sweeping your yard? That can't be good for your ankle. Do you know what you need?" she gave a broad smile. "You need a wife."

J.B.'s eyes shot to Delia's and they both blushed. Delia wished she was wearing her bonnet. She immediately busied herself with her soap.

"I know! Since you don't have a wife, you must visit my establishment so that my girls can care for you." Delia's head snapped up. Bertha's smile had broadened further, and she was looking J.B. up and down.

Delia stirred viciously, determined not to look at J.B. She didn't want to think of J.B. going to a place like that. She didn't want to know if he looked pleased by the suggestion. But, the silence. She couldn't help it. She looked. J.B. was red-faced, slowly shaking his head at Bertha. A little fountain of relief burst inside Delia. Until, Bertha turned to her.

"Are you sure you don't want to come work for me?"

Delia felt a tide of heat rush up her face, worse than before. She looked back and forth between J.B., who looked angry, and Big Bertha, who had a twinkle in her eye. That woman was stirring up trouble as clearly as Delia was stirring her pot. J.B. threw down his broom and stomped around his cabin and out of sight.

Delia couldn't speak. She was mortified to have had J.B. hear that. It didn't matter. Bertha spoke first.

"No matter, my dear. If you ever change your mind, you know where to find me." With that, Big Bertha flashed them both a naughty grin and sashayed out of the yard and down the road.

Delia watched Big Bertha go, noting the swinging of her velvet skirts and the men who turned to watch her walk away. She looked down at her own skirt, stained and dirty at the hem. She could feel how sweat-dampened her armpits were. Her skin was darkened by the sun all the way to where her sleeves were rolled back. Her hands were so cracked and red she had spots of blood on her knuckles. She pulled her bonnet back on, whether to protect her skin or simply hide, she wasn't sure.

Suddenly, a pile of clothes was slapped down on the board in front of her. "Don't forget to pay your rent." It was J.B.'s gruff voice. He had already turned away, limping out of the yard. "I'm going for a walk."

He did such a good job of acting like he didn't care about her, that in fact he might even dislike her, that sometimes she didn't think he was acting. Her heart drooped. He clearly did not like Big Bertha's suggestion that he get a wife.

Delia began to sort through the clothes he'd left. More laundry for tomorrow. She checked the pockets and felt a lump. She reached in and pulled out a sock wrapped around something. It was a small jar.

Mrs. Gripley's Hand Lotion.

Her heart soared. He did care. He noticed. *He cared.* She carefully slipped the jar into her pocket and whispered, "Thank you." Even though he wasn't there to hear her. She wanted to run after J.B., but she couldn't quite yet. She had to pour the soap liquid into the mold first.

And then she would find J.B.

Finished, she ran into her cabin to hang up her apron and smooth her hair. As she stepped outside, she saw a man standing at the juncture of the road and the path back to her laundry yard. He was wearing dungarees so encrusted with dirt that they looked like they could stand up even without a body inside them. His shirt collar was stained and he didn't wear a tie. He held a bundle of clothes under his arm. He was looking between the two cabins, unsure where to find the washerwoman.

She stopped in her tracks. The man looked at her. "Mrs. Watson?" Lots of men knew her name when they first came to her; she was one of only a few women in town. But he looked at her with recognition.

"Do I know you?"

"No ma'am. But I recognize you. Steven always carried a painted miniature of you. He took it out and looked at it whenever he was homesick. He was right proud of his pretty wife and loved to show you off to the other fellows."

Delia put her hand to her heart. Steven. She'd been thinking of the troubles in their marriage, and she'd forgotten the sweet man who courted her. Maybe his letters weren't just about control, but expressions of homesickness…it confused her.

He knew Steven. "Mr.…."

"Jonathon Cooper, ma'am."

"Mr. Cooper, do you know where Steven is?" She felt a little embarrassed. With the war over, she ought to know where her husband was. But she was not too embarrassed to ask. She needed to know.

Mr. Cooper's eyes widened. He took his hat off. "Mam, don't you know? He's dead."

Delia stumbled, and leaned against her worktable. She'd believed Steven dead, despite her recent fears, but still it was a shock to hear this man – this man who knew Steven – say it. Mr. Cooper rushed her side, ready to catch her if she fainted.

"Are you sure? Because, he's listed as missing. No one knows what happened."

Mr. Cooper looked startled. "Ah, gee, Mrs. Watson. I'm awfully sorry. I…I saw him. Wounded. Terrible gut wound. I couldn't stay with him. We was in the middle of battle and they was shootin'…but I can't imagine he survived that. No one could."

Delia deep breathed, fighting the darkness that wanted to encircle her. A gut wound. What a terrible injury. They said men would rather die outright than suffer one of those. "Are you sure?"

"As sure as I can be. Steven was my comrade and my friend. If I thought he'd had a chance of surviving I'd have gone back for him." His expression beseeched her. Mr. Cooper looked terribly worn down. Some men didn't recover after war, and he seemed to be one of them. He was unkempt, haggard, skinny. His eyes were hollow, shadowed.

She nodded. "Of course, you would have." She straightened up, the darkness at the edge of her vision fading. She took a deep breath.

"Do you have laundry for me, Mr. Cooper?"

Mr. Cooper gestured at the bundle he had dropped. "Well, I did, but I think maybe you need to go rest."

"Not at all. If I rest, then all I can do is think about Steven. I'd rather work." She took Mr. Cooper by the arm and ushered him toward the street. "Now, go down the road here, turn up there, and a little way down, you'll find a bath house. You go there tomorrow." She glanced at the sky. Clear. "You go there tomorrow. While you're bathing, have them run your dirty clothes back here. I'll have your clean ones ready."

Mr. Cooper nodded, but he still seemed a concerned for her. "I'm sorry. I…"

"Don't be sorry, Mr. Cooper. I needed to hear what you had to say." She watched him shuffle down the road, hat still in hand. Steven was probably dead. Probably. But then, what was happening here? She turned to the pile of laundry. She would have to talk to J.B. later. Maybe she was ready to tell him about her dilemma. She saw a movement out the corner of her eye. It was the dog.

"Go on, you," she said.

CHAPTER 26

J.B. meandered down the road, past the storefronts with their boardwalks, past the shacks and tents. With the thousands of men living and working around Virginia City, he was jostled several times. But he kept his head down and his hands in his pockets. He walked past the tailings and piles of dirt that made it look like the earth had been turned inside out.

While he walked, he remembered the calm stillness of Delia's bent head when she found the hand lotion he'd left for her. He'd stood just outside the yard, where she wouldn't notice him. Though he couldn't see her face, hidden by the sides of her blue bonnet, he did see her pull the small jar in close to her chest, as though hugging it tight, before dropping it into her apron pocket.

He found himself getting out of breath as he climbed the gentle hill toward his claim. Sitting around for a week had not been kind to him, but it hadn't been bad for his amputated foot which had enjoyed the rest. His other foot, the one he'd sprained, ached, but not so badly now. He didn't dare leave his claim unattended any longer. He'd had young Kit swing by a few times, and Chatty, too, but nothing protected a claim like being there.

He looked around the site, and it looked the same as the last time he'd seen it…but something didn't feel right. He had a suspicion that someone had been snooping around his claim. His tools were there, but it looked like someone had done a little digging. He couldn't know if they found anything, but it looked like he ought to start carrying his gun…though that was a sure sign to others that he had something to protect.

Last time he and Cal had hit it big, they'd taken turns sleeping at the mine until their payload ran out. He'd worked real hard to keep quiet and not tell anyone, but someone always figured it out. This time, it was only him working the mine, and he'd been stuck down in town because of his injury.

He spent some time pickaxing in the mineshaft, simply knocking out the earth, breaking down the walls. A little deeper, a little wider. Sometimes, he picked up a chunk of rock to study it. He chose some earth and ore that looked promising and put a shovelful in his rocker box. J.B. was hunched over, rocking the ore back and forth. Sweat wet a path down the back of his striped shirt, and his hair was damp around his face. Something glinted…something big, and he reached into the box. *Pop.* The sound of rock hitting another – such as when someone kicked one. His head jerked up.

Delia was approaching. She had pushed her bonnet off her head so it hung down her back. The sun kissed her light brown hair and she matched the autumn hillside. Relief and hope flooded him. No claim jumper. She'd come to him. She was seeking him out. His smile was involuntary, and it caused Delia to stop in her tracks.

"Oh, J.B.! You look a fright with that maniacal smile." She smiled back at him, uncertainly.

"Come on over. See what I've found."

She walked over and stood beside the rocker box. He

pointed with his finger. Among the gray brown rocks were little tiny flecks of golden rock, glinting in the sunlight. He took Delia's hand, turning it over to make a little cup with one hand. With other hand, he plucked a rock from the screen and carefully placed in her cupped palm. It was about the size of half a chicken's egg, encrusted with dirt but as Delia brushed it off, more and more of the gold shone in the sun.

"Oh, my goodness," she said in awe. Her green eyes sparkled and her sun-kissed cheeks perked into beautiful apples as she smiled. "Oh, J.B., this is it, isn't it? What you've been waiting for?"

He knew what he'd been waiting for, and the gold was only part of it.

"What are you going to do with it?" she asked. He looked at her eager face, and at her fingers wrapped around the nugget. The breeze whispered gently. J.B. raised his hand to gently brush a wind-strewn lock of hair off her face. He wrapped his own warm hands, calloused and dirty from the hard work, around her hand. Delia looked from the gold, held between both of their hands, to J.B.'s face.

"It would make a fine ring, don't you think?"

Delia pulled her hand away, twisting it to place the gold nugget back into his hand. She looked startled. In fact, she looked a deer caught unawares. J.B.'s heart sank.

"Why did you come here?" he bit out.

She flinched. "I...I, ah...I wanted to thank you for the lotion. That was very kind..." she petered out.

He stared at her.

"And, there was a man. He knew my husband...he was there..." She stopped. J.B. could tell there was more to her story. But he didn't care. He pulled out his poke bag of gold dust and added the nugget. He spent an inordinate amount of time tying it up. Delia turned around, heading back down the path to town. He willed himself to stay silent, but the question on his mind burst out. He called out.

"Are you not over your husband? Or are you heartbroken about Cal? Is that it? Because he can't marry you now."

She paused, her back to him. She turned her head so he could see her profile and considered his question. Her reply was a kick in the teeth.

"I only ever considered marrying Cal. No one else."

CHAPTER 27

Delia awoke soon after sunrise. She pulled her blanket tight up around her neck as she lay on her bunk, contemplating the soft light peeking through the shutters. Dawn was coming later and later. The extra sleep was nice, but the shorter days and cooler nights meant fall was here and winter not far behind.

Where she came from, late September was a beautiful season. The trees turned glorious red, orange and yellow. Cool nights were balanced with warm afternoons. It was fall, but the best kind of fall.

In Montana Territory, in the mountains, it was clear she was in for a long winter. The men were scrambling. Scrambling to work their mines as long as the water wasn't frozen. Scrambling to stock up, before the wagon trains stopped bringing in supplies for the winter. Her chatty customers had told her numerous times about the rioting last year, when Virginia City had run out of flour.

Anyone growing vegetables was harvesting or babying their gardens to eke out a little more growing time. Some men were telling stories about terrible storms. Some were talking about the card games and boredom to come. And some were high-tailing it south while the roads were still passable.

She had been wondering when her stove would arrive so J.B. could install it in her shack. But, now, she wondered instead if there was still time for her to hightail it with them. After yesterday, she didn't know how she could continue to live alongside J.B. She had gone to him to tell him about Steven, how she'd feared he might not be dead, that she wasn't a widow. Even with Mr. Cooper's last siting of her husband, she wasn't legally a widow. She'd wanted to come clean.

But she'd been so surprised by J.B.'s talk of a ring. She knew he cared, but she didn't expect him to be so forward so quickly. She didn't know how to respond when he didn't yet know her story, and she'd panicked. She realized that even if she told him, it wouldn't change anything. She would still be left in limbo, unable to move forward. How could they live like that?

Delia threw back her blanket and got out of bed. She shivered as she splashed water on her face, pressing the cold cloth around her eyes, hoping to reduce the puffiness that came from shedding so many tears during the night. She dressed in her work dress, put on her apron. These colder mornings meant it took even longer to heat the water for washing, so she liked to kindle the fire under the cauldron as early as possible. She smoothed her hair, drew her shawl around her shoulders, and opened the door.

There, on the flat stone that was her stoop, lay a dead rabbit. It was a brownish-gray, with a few hints of white as its fur prepared for winter. It looked like it had been caught in a snare.

She put her hands on the doorframe and stared down at it. Steven had brought her rabbits. He'd go out early, check his snares, and leave the rabbits on the door stoop, ready for her to skin them. She was flooded with memories. The first time, not long after they'd married, she'd mentioned how much she enjoyed rabbit stew. The next morning, he left a brace of rabbits on the stoop before he headed into the fields to work. She'd skinned them and made him a delicious stew. He'd declared it his favorite. She'd been so proud.

It was before he'd turned so controlling. Before he decided it wasn't his favorite, and insisted she change her recipe.

But this rabbit. It hadn't been processed or blooded. It looked like it was a few days old. It smelled. It was not a gift of love.

Delia felt like she had after Jimmy's legs had broken in the "accident." She was a widow who couldn't move on, unable to support herself, becoming fearful of the things going on around her. The subtle threats…and the not-so-subtle ones. In a moment of desperation, she'd gone to Cal's parents, to ask advice on how to move west on her own. It was his father who had suggested she go as a bride for Cal.

She looked at the rabbit, laying there on her stoop. It had to be from the same person who had taunted her in Missouri. Steven, or someone who had known him. Maybe a fellow soldier he'd spoken with. That other fellow here in Virginia City had heard about her from Steven, and even seen the miniature portrait he had brought to war.

She knew it.

She knew it.

She knew it.

And it made her angry.

She was done being scared. She was done running away.

Delia picked up the rabbit by the ears. It was past fresh. Not a proper gift. Not a nice gift.

The bears were getting ready to hibernate and had started showing up around town. She had to get the smelly carcass out there. She reached down and picked a rock off the edge of her wall. She slipped it into her pocket. She'd figure out what to do as she walked.

But first, she heard a scrabbling noise. Chatty's dog was under her wash bench, sniffing and pawing. She walked over and reached down to scratch behind his ears. He leaned into her one hand, ignoring the rabbit in her other.

"What good are you?" she whispered.

CHAPTER 28

J.B. walked out behind his cabin to see Delia standing in the yard. She had her hands on her hips and was studying the yard. She wasn't wearing her bonnet. Her hair, shiny and brown, framed her pretty face, which was wearing a frown.

He wished he could have avoided her, but he hadn't realized she'd returned from wherever she'd gone early this morning. He knocked on the side of the cabin. Delia gave a little jump and laid her hand on her chest.

"Oh, J.B., you startled me!" Her face turned pale, except two flaming patches of red on her cheeks. He realized then that she hadn't started her wash fire, that there was no laundry in progress.

"Is everything all right?" he asked.

"Yes," she said with an emphatic nod, the color returning to her face. Then, she switched to shake of her head. "Well, no." She had her hands back on her hips.

He liked seeing Delia with this fire in her eyes. It was better than the scared deer look she'd worn yesterday. But it didn't make sense.

"Care to explain?" he asked.

"There was a dead rabbit on my stoop this morning."

A dead rabbit? "Did it look sick?"

"No, it had been trapped and left there," she said with gritted teeth.

"One of your admirers?"

"Not exactly." She took a deep breath and J.B. felt as though he was about hear something momentous. And then, he did. "You are in danger. I might be, too."

"Care to explain?" he asked yet again.

"I will, J.B. But when I'm done, you may not want me here. I'll leave here, if you want, but not Virginia City. I'm not going to run again."

J.B. didn't know whether he was in danger, or what was going on, but he was glad to see Delia was done feeling scared. He hated the circles under her eyes, her jumpiness, and knowing she was waiting for…something. He admired the calm determination in Delia's countenance. This was no panicked response to a dead rabbit. She had a fire burning inside her that made her green eyes turn gray around the edges, like a storm cloud moving in.

And she wasn't hiding behind that damn bonnet.

"Hang on," J.B. said, "I'll bring chairs out." He reentered his cabin and grabbed the two chairs each by its rail. He placed them along the back wall of his cabin, where Delia and he could see the path to the creek but not be seen by someone walking by on the road in front.

He gave a fancy bow and held his hands out, as if he was offering Delia a golden throne. The fire in her eyes calmed. He liked how her eyes creased when she was genuinely pleased, as if her cheeks had decided to move north.

She sat in the chair farther from the path. He took the other chair. The sun shone on them, but it was surrounded by clouds and did little to warm the brisk morning air. Delia's brown hair was shiny and smooth against her head. It was gathered at the base of her neck. J.B. imagined pulling the pins and seeing her hair falling into long tendrils.

He realized Delia was watching him watch her.

"No bonnet this morning," he stated, hoping she wouldn't realize what had really been on his mind.

"No bonnet ever," she said with a shrug. "I'm not hiding anymore."

"Sooo," he asked, "Does this mean we can stop pretending to dislike each other?"

Delia gave him a rueful smile. "Yes. I'm sorry I've made everything so difficult. I'll try to explain." But then she paused, and so J.B. gave voice to the question he'd been wondering for a while. "Delia, did your husband really die in the War, or did you run away?" She wouldn't be the first woman to escape a bad marriage by running away. He was determined to help her, but he wanted to know what he was up against.

Delia looked startled. "What? Oh. I —" Yet another deep breath. "I thought he was dead. I thought he was killed in battle. But his uncle didn't want to admit it; he loved him too much."

"There was no body?" J.B. asked.

"No body," she agreed. She gave a shiver in the cool air. "And then someone started causing me trouble… trouble that was connected to Steven… trouble that caused an innocent boy to be injured. So, I came out here, to start over. I thought Cal would understand that I might not be a widow…that he wouldn't care."

J.B. sat quietly, looking up at the gathering gray clouds.

"And then Cal didn't want to marry me. And I realized I couldn't force that uncertainty on…anyone else." She glanced at J.B. then. He stayed quiet.

"Then this man, this fellow soldier, came by. He told me he was certain Steven was dead…but he hadn't actually seen it so. Even so, I got hopeful again."

She reached over and put her hand on J.B.'s arm. "When you spoke yesterday, it scared me. I was getting a bit hopeful, but I realized that I still didn't know. I didn't know to admit it to you. And with trouble starting again, I didn't want you to get hurt."

J.B. nodded. He didn't move his arm. But he did ask, "So, you're not holding a candle for your husband? Or Cal?"

"What? No, not Steven. Not Cal." Decisive. Emphatic.

Excitement filled him and he wanted to jump up off the chair, but Delia twisted in her seat and gripped J.B.'s arm. "The thing is, this rabbit this morning. That's Steven. I'm sure of it. I don't know how he survived, or why he didn't come home. But it's him." The fire returned to her eyes. "But I'm not going to live like this. I'm not."

J.B. put his hand on top of Delia's hands, still locked around his forearm. He gave her a gentle squeeze. "I think you know how I feel about you, Delia." He took a deep breath. "I can live with the uncertainty of your widowhood. But I'm not going to have you terrorized. I'm going to protect you."

Delia's eyes were wide, inches from his. She gave him a tremulous smile.

"Really, J.B?" she whispered.

He didn't know if she was asking about him protecting her, or how he felt about her widowhood, or how he felt about her, but it didn't matter. The answer was the same.

"Really," he said. And then, right there in the yard, with no broad-brimmed hats or bonnets, where anyone could see them, he leaned over and pressed his lips to hers. And she kissed him back.

CHAPTER 29

"Good afternoon, Mrs. Watson," a voice boomed. It was Chatty Dawson, dimpled cheeks shining over his newly-trimmed beard. He looked clean and crisp and a far cry from how he'd looked the last time she saw him. Even the handkerchief in his pocket lay flat and posed.

"Chatty," said Delia with a smile. She took the stick she was using to stir the tub of clothes and laid it aside. She put her hands on her aching back and said, "Good afternoon to you, too. You clean up nicely."

She laughed when Chatty held out his hands as though holding a skirt and gave a small curtsy, all the while batting his lashes and simpering like a debutante. "Oh, Chatty! You are a card."

Chatty straightened. "Don't worry. I don't have a second laundress. I bought these new duds from Reggie at the Mercantile. Nice fella. They're just right, except a little long in the leg. Or, I'm a little short in the shank."

Delia laughed again. She turned to her shelf that J.B. had put up along the side of her cabin. She took the neat stack of clothes, tied together with twine, and carried it over to Chatty.

He took the stack and at the same time presented her with a pretty green ribbon.

"Thank you kindly, Mrs. Watson," he said. Perhaps seeing the question in her eyes, he lowered his voice. "This here is for you to put in your hair and show it off to your other admirers. I think at least one – J.B. for instance – might step up if he gets to thinking some other fella might sweep you away."

Delia felt the blood rushing to flame her face. "Oh, no. J.B. doesn't—. I'm not—" She ran her fingers over the soft material.

"Now, don't tell me that, Mrs. Watson. It's common knowledge you two are sweet on each other, but you're both holding back." Delia raised her head in astonishment. *What?* He couldn't know what held her back, but *common knowledge?* And she thought she'd been protecting J.B. with her acting skills.

Chatty stepped a little closer and lowered his voice a little more. "Take some advice from an old codger. It's terrible losing your wife – or husband, in your case – but if you wait too long, it becomes harder and harder to move on. You don't want to grow old alone." His eyes unfocused as he looked into his long past. Then, he shook his head and looked at Delia again.

Delia put her hand on Chatty's wrist. "I'm sorry, Chatty." She didn't say sorry for your loss, for your wife's death, or for being alone and lonely. She meant it all and knew he understood.

"Over time," he said, "you forget all the bad stuff—the arguments and struggles – and you only remember the good times." His eyes took on a shine. He closed them and shook his head. When he opened them, he had that humorous twinkle back. He started waggling his brows. "And the lovin'. Can't forget that!"

He started laughing a big booming laugh. Delia leaned up and gave him a kiss on the cheek. Chatty stopped laughing and his rosy cheeks bloomed brighter. Delia stepped back and waggled her own eyebrows at Chatty. They both laughed. Chatty tipped his hat.

Then, Chatty adjusted his bundle of clothes to carry more easily. Just before Delia turned back to her laundry, Chatty leaned over and whispered, "Save those kisses for J.B. I'm a little old for you. He's 'bout the right age." He winked and headed out of the yard and down the lane.

Delia shook her head. She was red-faced from laughing and embarrassment. She wondered if others really thought as Chatty did, that she and J.B. were sweet on each other. She lost her smile, wondering if anyone – if Steven – had seen her kiss J.B. the day before. She had jumped up immediately, told him they couldn't do that again. Not until it was safe. She wasn't going to hide behind the bonnet anymore, but she didn't want to put J.B. in danger either. Two broken legs would ruin him.

She wondered if kissing Chatty, which she'd done without thought, would take the sting out of her kiss with J.B. Maybe she should start kissing all her customers. How far did she need to go? She was going to end up working at Bertha's at this rate.

She realized she still held the ribbon in her hand. She needed to place it safely inside her cabin before she returned to work.

CHAPTER 30

"Hey, J.B.!"

J.B. looked up to see Reggie waving him over to the store porch. J.B. trudged up the road, worn from a long day digging and rocking for gold. It had been fruitless today. His back ached. His hands ached. His ankles ached. And all for nothing. He knew it was there. He felt in his gut that it was close. But not yet.

"If your face was any longer, you'd be a hound dog," said Reg.

"I feel about that good," said J.B. He leaned against the porch post and dropped his rucksack. "Was there something you wanted or did you just miss my pretty face?"

"Pretty to a blind man, yes," said Reggie automatically, without humor. He then took a moment to look around, to make sure no one was close enough to overhear the two men. J.B. pushed away some of his exhaustion.

"What?"

"Chatty Dawson?"

J.B. nodded. "I know him."

"Shot dead."

J.B.'s head recoiled. Chatty Dawson was a talkative fellow, hiring on for jobs whenever he could get them. He'd make enough money to drink and gamble, lose it all, and have to start over. But he was an amiable man and no threat to anyone.

J.B. grabbed his hat from his head and slapped it against his thigh. A cloud of dust arose. "What is wrong with this place?"

Reggie didn't answer. He gave the tiniest of shrugs. "Accused of cheating."

J.B. frowned at Reggie. "I find that hard to believe."

Reggie nodded. "A lot of men feel the same. But the shooter didn't hang around to discuss it. He slipped out in the melee."

"That's a damn shame." J.B. shook his head, as though to shake away the terrible image. "Anyone we know?"

"No, I don't think so," said Reggie. "It was a newcomer. But that's why I wanted to make sure you knew. The fellow's name might have been Wasser. Or Watson."

At that J.B. stilled. Watson?

"I know Chatty liked to visit with your Mrs. Watson, and he brought her gifts a few times. I couldn't help but wonder, after the troubles she'd had, if there could be a connection." With Reggie's law background, J.B. knew he ought to be concerned.

"What did this Watson look like?"

Reggie shook his head. "No one is quite sure. A little thick in the middle. He wore a hat."

J.B. looked out at the men walking and riding the road in front of Reggie's store. So many men showing up every day. No way to track them. No way to find a needle in the haystack when he didn't even have a description of the needle.

His brain was churning like a water wheel and he forgot about his exhaustion.

"Thanks, Reggie. Let me know if you hear anything else. I better get back to Delia."

Reggie nodded. J.B. picked up his rucksack and threw it over his shoulder as he stepped off the porch.

145

Delia looked up to see J.B. striding toward her. She began to smile until she noticed his grim expression. She put down the iron and stepped away from the shirt she'd been working on.

"J.B.?"

As soon as he reached her, he grabbed Delia's hands in his. "Any trouble today?"

Delia was startled by J.B.'s open show of concern. They had been slowly, sweetly, revealing their feelings, but not that anyone else could see. Not after that kiss.

She shook her head. She could see he was tense, but somehow, she was having trouble taking her focus away from his warm, callused hands wrapped around hers. She wondered how he could be thinking of anything else.

And then her ears finally heard what he was saying.

"Chatty? Dead?"

"I'm afraid so," J.B. said.

Delia could only picture the sweet, sloppy man who would come by to drop off an armload of laundry and stay for an hour telling her stories about his week. He had a way of pursing his lips and crinkling in his eyes which always tipped her off that his stories were about to become tall tales. He was a kind man. *Was.*

J.B. gave her hands a squeeze. "The thing is, Delia, he was shot by a fellow that accused him of cheating. Someone named Wassner. Or Watson."

She knew immediately what J.B. was saying. Her greatest fear, that her husband was still alive and haunting her, rose up inside her like a wriggling snake. She didn't know how he could be when he'd been seen to be fatally injured. She didn't know why he wouldn't have just come home or come to her here in Virginia City if he was alive. She didn't know anything except history seemed to be repeating itself. Someone who was kind and sweet to her was a victim under suspicious circumstances. But this time, the victim wasn't injured. He was dead. *Chatty was dead.*

Delia jerked backward, ripping her hands out of J.B.'s. She stumbled back, trying to put distance between them. She felt her breath quickening. It was too late. She had held hands with J.B. openly. *She had kissed him.* She grabbed her apron, wringing it in her hands, trying to squeeze away the terror.

J.B. stepped toward her. "Don't worry. I won' t let anything happen to you."

"You don't understand. It's not me I'm concerned about. It's you." A loud sob escaped. "It's you."

J.B. tried to touch her shoulder but she whirled away. "Yesterday, Chatty brought me a ribbon. And I kissed him on the cheek. If he hadn't – If I hadn't—" she broke off. "Don't touch me!"

She saw the disappointment on J.B.'s face, that she wouldn't let him comfort her. And the resolve, his determination to help her. Which was the worst thing she could think of.

She ran into her cabin and closed the door.

She looked around the one room, at the table and the bunk

she slept on. Up until recently, this little space had been her refuge. Smaller than her old home, but bigger in freedom. And lying there at night, knowing J.B. was so close by, had given her a sense of security she hadn't felt in years. Surrounded by thousands of people, mostly men, mostly strangers, but safe in her own little nest. That sense of security had been fading with the small vandalisms and invasions, but now it was gone. She knew that every night she would strain her ears, listening for Steven coming for J.B.

And that would never be enough. J.B. might be alone at his mine, or just walking down the street, and a surprise attack could do him in. He would never be safe with her.

Delia's heart squeezed until it shattered.

She loved J.B. She loved him with a passion she never thought possible. She couldn't even call it complete, because the love felt never-ending. There were no boundaries to it. No end. It washed over her and through her and out into the world. Over the mountains and up to the sky.

She sank to her knees, onto the braided rag rug covering the dirt floor, and pushed her fists into her eyes. No tears, she willed. No tears, for those, too, would be never-ending.

CHAPTER 32

The sound of the dirt falling onto the coffin made J.B. flinch. There was something about that first shovelful – it echoed on the wood. The men kept shoveling dirt into the hole, until the sound was muffled, dirt on dirt, and the only other sound was the panting breaths of Chatty's friends. It didn't feel quite right to J.B., burying Chatty in Boot Hill Cemetery just down from the road agents buried there. It seemed wrong to bury a good man like Chatty next to criminals like that. He shivered, noting the snowflakes starting to fall from the gray clouds.

One of the men called out, "Anyone here good at carving?"

J.B. hesitated, but no one else responded. "I'm not the finest woodworker, but I can do it."

The man nodded. "I've got a nice piece of oak, part of a wagon I'm dismantling. I'll drop it by your place." J.B. took a moment to get the details on Chatty's birth year and true name for the grave marker he would carve. And then he walked off alone.

Delia had already left to walk down the hill with Big Bertha. She'd refused to walk with him. He was concerned for her safety, but she was concerned for his. She was certain Chatty was dead because of her. J.B. was worried about this but couldn't be entirely sure. Chatty had been a likeable fellow, and there were no indications he was a card cheat, but then, J.B. had only known him to say hello. He'd never played cards with him. He didn't really know him. He didn't really know what had caused someone to shoot him. But, given all that had happened, it was suspicious.

J.B. left the cemetery and headed down the hill, back into town. He was at a loss. He'd do anything to protect Delia. He stopped.

He'd do anything to protect Delia.

He had known that he cared about Delia. His feelings for her had been growing since he met her. He had thought she would make a fine bride and wife. But this protective/possessive/all-encompassing emotion he felt for Delia was like nothing he'd ever felt before. He wanted her. He wanted to protect her. He wanted to be with her and love her.

He loved her. He loved her with all of his being. J.B. took off at a fast clip. He wanted to shout his love to the world. And he was going to do just that. He was going to draw out Steven and end this.

CHAPTER 33

Delia sat on the edge of her bunk with her purse on her lap. She counted all her coins and bills. It was enough to get a stage out of town, down to Utah, surely. Could she make it all the way to California? Or perhaps Seattle? If she left before the snows hit... She'd have to check the stagecoach schedule.

But it wasn't enough to start over. She hefted her small poke bag of gold nuggets and dust. Most men paid for their laundry services in gold and she had what she collected from the wash water. She wasn't sure how much it was worth. Enough, she hoped, to help her set up. She needed to visit the Assayer's office. She needed not to get robbed on her way south.

Would there be such a need for a laundress outside a mining town? Perhaps she should aim for another one.

Delia then turned to the knife. It was small and sharp, with a pearl handle. Bertha had given it to her. After Chatty's funeral, they had spoken at length. Delia had told Bertha everything. The woman had told her she'd have Kit stop by once a day.

"You send a message if need be," Big Bertha had said.

Delia hesitated. She thought of Jimmy and his broken legs. Bertha had seen her indecision and pressed the small knife into her hand.

"I've got one already," Delia had told her, patting her pocket.

"Good," said Bertha, "Now you have two. They never expect that from a woman."

And that was why Delia was sitting here, wondering. What did Steven expect from her? If he wouldn't come out in the open, how long did he think this cat and mouse game could go on? She could run away, hoping to protect J.B. But she didn't want to leave J.B.

Bang. Bang. "Mrs. Watson! Mrs. Watson!" It was young Kit, banging on her door.

Delia jumped up. She threw a blanket over her savings and then unbarred the door. "What is it, Kit?"

The boy was gasping for breath. "Big Bertha sent me. I ran all the way! Mr. Wood is going all over town, telling everyone and anyone that he's gonna marry you. He's goin' to his claim to dig up some gold to make you a big ring, he said."

Delia's hand rose to her lips. She pressed them, as though grounding herself in reality. "This is…this is not good."

Kit, whose breath was returning to normal, cocked his head. "You don't want to marry him?"

She didn't answer. She ran back inside, grabbed the knife Big Bertha had given her and slipped it into her pocket. She looked around for another weapon. Since she'd be noticed carrying a big pan in her hands, she instead took a sock filled with soap slivers and put that in another pocket. If she swung the sock at someone's head it would be quite an impact. She grabbed her shawl and ran back out the door, slamming it behind her.

"Thank you, Kit!" she yelled as she hightailed it out of the yard. She walked briskly. Boy, was she going to have a word with J.B! He couldn't just decide to antagonize Steven. Did he think it was as simple as that? Steven would just walk up to them and say, "Hey now, I'm her husband." She balled her fists as she walked. She rushed down the boardwalk, men tipping their hats as she passed. She ignored them all.

As Delia reached the edge of town, she realized she had been following the same route as a man. As the crowds thinned out, she realized the blue shirt and beat-up brown hat had been in front of her for two blocks. The man was walking furtively, glancing around often. He paused and turned to look down an alley, revealing his profile. It was Freddy. She slowed down, not wanting to interact with him. But she kept going, because it was the same direction.

Delia hesitated. She needed to get to J.B. *Get to J.B.* Freddy started off again, and he was headed in the direction of J.B.'s claim. Was Freddy their troublemaker? Delia held back, following at a distance. Was he headed for J.B.? Was J.B.'s plan this immediately effective? Questions swirled in Delia's head. She had been sure it was Steven…had she been so wrong?

She stopped again and looked around. There, leaning against the false front of a bar, was Michael Flaherty. He looked like he had been in conversation with the man next to him, but he had stopped and was looking right at her. He pushed away from the wall and walked toward Delia when she called out to him.

"Mr. Flaherty! Michael!"

"Mrs. Watson? You look riled up," he said.

"I need your help, please," she said hurriedly. She looked over his shoulder, trying not to lose sight of Freddy in the distance. "J.B. has done something foolish."

Michael gave her a wry smile. "That won't be the first time."

"I'm serious! He's trying to draw out the man who has been stalking me. And I think he's succeeded."

Michael stilled. "Is that so?"

"I need you to…to get Reg Smith, at the Merc. Bring him with you to J.B.'s claim. I think Freddy is headed to J.B. right now." She craned her neck, trying to spot Freddy in the distance. She'd lost sight of him. She glanced back at Michael Flaherty. His usual smile was missing. He was staring at her intently, assessing. Well, she didn't have time to explain. "Please hurry!"

Without waiting for a response, she took off down the dusty road, running until she saw Freddy again. She'd have to hope Michael and Reg showed up in time.

Delia tried to stay at a distance, so that Freddy wouldn't notice her. She had hoped she might be wrong, but then he turned onto the trail that led toward J.B.'s mine. She glanced back, but there was no sign of Michael and Reg following yet. It didn't matter. She didn't want Freddy to sneak up on J.B. She lifted her skirts and jogged after Freddy.

Ahead, the trail split. Her last bit of hope rested on whether Freddy took the branch toward J.B. or the other that led in a different direction. She peered around a rock and saw Freddy had chosen neither. He was standing there. Waiting. He looked around, mostly in the direction of that other trail. Then, in the trees beyond him, she saw a movement. Freddy saw it too and walked into the shadows.

He was speaking with a man, pointing up the hill in J.B.'s direction. She couldn't see the other man well. He wore a hat and stood in the shadows. But there was something about him…something that seemed familiar. She watched as the man gripped Freddy's shoulder. Shook it. Whatever he was saying, Freddy nodded.

The two men turned and emerged from the shadows. With his broad-rimmed hat, she still couldn't see the identity of the second man. He was dressed like a miner, but cleaner. He hadn't been digging or panning in that outfit. The two men returned to the trail…heading toward J.B. Delia's heart stilled. The way that man walked…her heart started racing.

She glanced back, but still no sign of the cavalry. She wished she had time to run back for help. But she feared it was too late for that.

She waited until the men disappeared over the crest of the trail and then hightailed it after them. She yanked her skirt when it snagged a sagebrush and heard it rip. She tripped over a rock and stumbled. *Get a hold of yourself*, she thought. She slowed at the crest, not wanting to rush into full view of the men. She approached a bluff, trying to peer around the edge carefully. She saw Freddy, standing in the middle of the trail, with his hands in his pockets. Where was the other man?

She felt the press of cold metal against her neck.

CHAPTER 34

J.B. sat on a cut log, using it as a stool. He leaned over his rocker box, running his fingers through the ore, looking for gold. He was waiting. There was a hum in his head, a feeling of anticipation. It reminded him of the calm before a battle. The men knew the enemy was near and it was only a matter of time before the fighting began.

He remembered his first battle. He'd felt this same hum, just before the air around the soldiers had begun whistling the sound of mortar shells. The Union Army had shown up with dozens of rifled cannons and rained down shells on the Confederate men.

J.B. pulled himself out of his memory. He was staring at his rocks, but not paying any attention. He'd set a trap but wasn't looking for his prey. He sat still and listened carefully. He heard nothing – a stillness that was unnatural. He slowly began to rise, sliding his hand toward his gun. Before he could reach it, Freddy appeared on the trail, already aiming a gun at J.B.

Damn, thought J.B., one moment of distraction and they got the drop on me.

"I wouldn't do that, J.B." Freddy smiled an unfriendly smile. "Yeah, I know your name. I know lots about you. Like, you're sweet on this girl." He pointed with his thumb over his shoulder, and around the bend came Delia. She was pale under her tan, wringing her hands as she walked. An older man had a gun trained at her back, prompting her up the trail. He was the stout fellow that J.B. had seen outside the yard with Freddy that one time.

They stopped just outside J.B.'s work area. The older man stepped up next to Delia. He grabbed her upper arm with one hand while the other continued to aim the gun at her.

J.B. looked at Delia. "Alright there?"

She gave a brief nod, her eyes sliding sideways toward the man beside her. He didn't say a word but maintained his proprietary grip. J.B. leaned toward them but before he could do anything, Freddy cocked his gun and said, "You can stay right there, J.B., but toss your gun over here."

Once he had the gun, Freddy relaxed. He stood midway between Delia and J.B. "Well, now, it's time to settle up." He pointed his gun toward the mine pit. "I know you have a big ol' chunk of gold you've been excavating. Trying to hide it in a slag pile. But I've been sleuthing."

J.B. felt his jaw drop. He'd been sure that his hiding place was a secret. He'd been unable to secure the site. He was kicking himself.

"And if I get this for you, you'll let Delia go?"

"What!?" Freddy laughed. "No, no! This gold is my payment – for services rendered. You'll have to talk to Mr. Watson about pretty Ms. Delia."

J.B.'s head snapped to the man beside Delia. "Steven Watson?"

Delia gave the slightest shake of her head. "No. Steven's uncle."

The man's lips stretched into a slow, menacing smile. "Gold first," he said.

J.B. was almost glad to start dragging the debris away from the hole. His mind was racing and he needed time to think. *Uncle Geoffrey.* He thought back over the stories Delia had told him about Steven and realized how many of them also featured Steven's uncle. Was this really just about gold? Freddy had said it was his payment. So, what was Geoffrey's?

He strained to lift a large rock out of the hole, dropping to the ground, to the hole. He grabbed his shovel. Freddy still had a gun trained on him and Geoffrey still had a gun trained on Delia. He stuck the shovel in the dirt and began excavating. He tried to draw it out.

"No lollygagging there," said Freddy.

J.B. looked up at him, and then to Geoff. "Steven. Is he with you? Is he alive?"

Geoff gave that slow, creepy smile again, the kind a snake would make if a snake could smile. "Wouldn't you like to know?"

J.B. stopped shoveling. "Well, yes."

Freddy looked back and forth between them. "Who's Steven?"

Geoff pointed to the hole. "Keep working." J.B. shuffled his shovel around but couldn't take his eyes off the scene in front of him. Geoff turned to Delia, one hand pointing his gun into her side, the other tucking loose hairs behind her ear. "Steven was my nephew. And he was Delia's husband."

"Was?" J.B. asked forcefully, wanting to distract Geoff, hating his touching Delia. She was leaning away from him, trying to get out of reach of his fingers.

Geoff answered him, but he never took his eyes, or his hand off Delia. "Was, I'm sure. He would have come home to us."

Delia was looking sideways at Geoffrey, alarmed by the way he said "us." The way he drew it out, lovingly. J.B. started to step out of the hole, but he heard the cocking of a gun. It was Freddy's. "Don't."

Geoff's hand drifted down Delia's neck, to her collar. He gently straightened it. "He's gone, but we have each other. I know it's hard to learn you're a widow, but now you can move on. I'll take care of you. You'll learn to love me."

Delia shuddered. "Is that why you tried so hard to make me think Steven was alive? So I couldn't move on?"

Geoff shrugged. "I wasn't sure about him at first, either."

J.B. was vibrating with the need to rush Geoffrey, to shove him away from Delia, to pound him into the ground for touching her. For terrorizing her. For trying to take her away from him. Only Geoff's gun, pressed into Delia's side, and Freddy's gun aimed at him, stopped him.

J.B. cussed. "It's here. Right here." He gestured to a burlap bag on the ground. He pulled it off, dirt and pebbles falling to the side. And there was a beautiful, shiny, enormous chunk of gold ore. It was about the size of half a bucket. There were streaks of gray and black granite, but with more gold throughout than any other big piece of ore that J.B. had ever found. It was everything he had ever dreamed of. Everything he had hoped for. It was what kept him going through this backbreaking work.

And he'd give it up happily if it meant keeping Delia safe.

But he was afraid that wasn't enough. He knew his last chance to rescue her was coming, when the men would be distracted by the gold. Even if Geoff was giving it all to Freddy, he'd have to be impressed. And maybe it was enough that he wouldn't want to give it all. J.B. could incite a fight.

He reached down to haul it out, his arms and back straining to lift it. He shoved it onto the ledge.

He prepared to spring out of the hole, right at Freddy. He

turned his head to catch Delia's eye, willing her to be ready. Her eyes widened, but they weren't looking at him. They were looking behind him.

Pain exploded in the back of his head and everything went dark.

CHAPTER 35

Delia screamed as J.B. crumpled, disappearing into the hole. She tried to rush forward, but Geoff grabbed her arm, holding it tight, and shoved the muzzle of the gun under her ribs.

"I've had enough of your misbehaving. You'll do as I say, or I'll put you down like a rabid dog." His voice was deep and rough and like nothing she'd ever heard him utter before. Chills ran down her spine. She stood still, waiting. She wouldn't let them shoot J.B. She had to get them out of here.

"Let's leave now. Right now. All of us," she said. She took a deep breath. "And I won't give you any more trouble."

Geoffrey squeezed her upper arm until she thought he might break it. "You don't think I see where your hand is inching to?" He let go of her arm and reached into her pocket, pulling out a knife.

"Please—" she gasped. He shoved her forward and she fell to her knees.

"Freddy!" Geoffrey barked. "You're not leaving with that gold until we're sure J.B. can't follow." Freddy swung around with his gun aimed down into the hole.

"No!" screamed Delia.

Geoffrey kicked her in the side at the same time as he yelled at Freddy, "No! Damn fool! We've made it this far without getting noticed. No gunshots unless absolutely necessary." He walked over and picked up the shovel. "Fill it."

Delia watched as Freddy's face turned sour. He holstered his gun and took the shovel. He used it to point at Delia. "She can help."

Delia felt her heart stutter at the idea of burying J.B., like her very insides were being crushed. Still on her knees, she put her clasped hands to her chest. "Please, no."

Geoff grabbed her hair and tilted her head back. "If you'd rather, we can slit his throat and leave. I'd prefer something less obvious, in case anyone comes looking around, but it's up to you."

Delia's eyes watered until Geoffrey was a blurred image, inches from her face. She whispered, "No. I'll help." She wasn't sure she could help J.B., but she'd try.

She grabbed the burlap sack and slid into the hole. J.B. was half sitting, half lying against the side. She pulled on his arm until he slid all the way down, lying with his head next to an outcropping of rock. She threw the burlap sack over him, trying to catch it on the rocks around his head. She was trying to create an air pocket. She leaned down and whispered, "I love you, J.B."

"What're you doing?" Freddy asked.

"I'm showing respect. Haven't you ever buried anyone before?" she spat out. If she acted like he was dead already, if they thought he was dead, maybe they wouldn't try so hard to ensure it.

Freddy answered with a shovelful of dirt that rained down over her and the burlap-covered J.B. Delia scrambled to protect J.B. without appearing to do so. She pulled larger rocks off the ledge, sliding them down the side and arranging them next to

J.B.'s prone form. She tried to not to let anything too big or heavy land on him. She wished he'd wake up. She feared he'd wake up. Geoffrey was pacing, frequently looking down the trail to see if anyone was coming. Freddy kept dumping dirt and pebbles over J.B., slowly covering his body, getting it all over Delia's dress and hair, too. When neither man was paying attention, she arranged the rocks and burlap around J.B.'s head, trying to create breathing holes. When there was enough dirt that it wasn't obvious there was a body, she said, "How long are we going to stay here?"

Freddy paused his digging. Both he and Geoffrey peered into the hole.

"I'm finished," said Freddy. "This is good enough. Now, I told you I'd get you out of Virginia City, but if you don't leave now, the deal's off."

Geoffrey's gun hand swung toward Freddy and for a moment, he didn't say anything. Delia thought Geoffrey was going to shoot him. From the way Freddy's eyes widened, he thought so, too. Instead, the gun moved again, to aim at Delia. "Help her out."

Freddy reached a hand down. Delia grabbed it and allowed him to pull her out of the hole. Once on level ground again she looked back down at the mound that was J.B. She flinched when Freddy kicked the shovel; it landed on J.B. He didn't move a muscle.

Freddy emptied out J.B.'s rucksack. He rolled the ore into it and wrestled it onto his back. "This way." He took off walking down the trail. Geoff waved his gun in Delia's face, then shoved her to follow. It was cold. She slid her hands into her pockets. A few snowflakes fell from the sky.

CHAPTER 36

J.B.'s head throbbed. He was weighed down, far from light and sound. He simply lay still, trying to accommodate the pain swimming at the back of his head. He tried to open his eyes, but it was dim and he couldn't figure out where he was. Muffled sound began to work its way through his ears. He tried to lift his arms, to push the cobwebs from his eyes, but he couldn't. He couldn't move. He couldn't see. He couldn't hear. He couldn't even take a deep breath. He began to panic, trying to thrash about though he wasn't sure he was actually moving.

Suddenly, something was pulled off his head and bright light blinded him and cold air made him cough. His skull spiked pain and he felt a wave of nausea. He closed his eyes and stilled himself. Finally, he tried to make sense of the noise around him.

He looked up and saw a dog's face peering at him from a distance. It was whining.

"J.B., can you hear me? J.B., it's me, Reg."

"And Michael Flaherty," another voice said.

J.B. moved his eyes just a little. Through the slits, he realized what was happening. He was at the bottom of his pit, half buried. Reg and Michael were digging him out. Chatty's dog was dancing around the cusp of the hole. It was so bright because he was on his back, staring straight up into the light gray sky.

"Delia," he coughed out.

Reg didn't pause as he shoved dirt and rock off J.B.'s arms. "She's not here. She was headed this way. Did she make it?"

J.B. gave a weak nod. He willed himself to ignore the pain.

Michael, working on uncovering his legs, asked, "Was it her husband? He's still alive?"

"No," said J.B. "Steven's uncle. Geoffrey Watson. Working with Freddy." He used his one free arm to push dirt-encrusted hair off his face. "They've got Delia. We've got to get to her."

Reg took J.B.'s arm and pulled him into sitting position. Dirt and pebbles cascaded from his shirt. He struggled to break his legs free as his two friends continued to use their hands to shovel dirt away. They helped him get to his feet and out of the hole. His head throbbed, but it didn't matter. He needed to get to Delia. They went down the trail, pausing at the split. Which way?

"I'll go to town for more men," said Michael. "There'll be plenty willing to help look for Miss. Delia. If I see any signs this way, I'll run back and let you know."

"I can help you track," said Reg.

J.B. nodded slowly. "I think this dog can help, too." Chatty's dog had started off down the trail away from town. He was stopped, nosing around the trail. Suddenly, he licked the ground. J.B. walked over and got down on one knee. "Can you smell Delia, li'l fellow? Can you track her?" He ran his hand down the dog's back.

The dog lurched forward and licked his face. J.B. jerked his head back, but then leaned forward and sniffed. He looked up at the other two men and smiled. "Delia's pine soap. She's leaving a trail."

It was evening. Delia, Freddy and Geoffrey had walked until it was nearly dark. Freddy had led them to a man-made cave; it was an abandoned pit mine. Now, they sat in the dark with a small fire for warmth. Freddy hadn't wanted a fire, said it was too easy to find them, but Geoffrey had insisted. He wasn't used to roughing it and, he'd said, "My bride mustn't catch sick because of this adventure." His voice was back to the sickly sweet one, and Delia wasn't sure if her shivers came from the voice or the cold.

It was snowing outside, a heavy, unseasonable – according to Freddy – snow. They'd arrived in time to the cave that there would be no footprints uncovered to show their way, though how they'd leave in the morning, no one was discussing. Unfortunately, Delia's scented lye soap trail, questionable at best, was a failure. No one would notice a sliver of white soap resting under the snow.

She pulled her shawl closer around, staring into the fire. Suddenly, a shadowy movement in the corner of her eye caught her attention. Unfortunately, it caught Freddy's, too. He immediately pulled out his gun, cocking it. Geoffrey's head snapped to attention. All three sets of eyes were glued to the dark entrance of the cave.

A shot rang out, the sound echoing around them. Freddy staggered back, red blooming from his shoulder, his gun flying from his hand. It discharged as it hit the ground, shards of rock splintering through the air. Geoffrey fumbled for his gun, but before he could unholster it, J.B. dove into the cave and tackled him. Delia scrambled to get out of the way. They rolled toward the fire, and away from it, punching each other.

Delia heard a grunt and saw Freddy stumbling toward J.B. and Geoffrey. She reached into her pocket and pulled out Bertha's knife. It was small, but sharp. She shuttled across the ground like a spider and plunged the knife into Freddy's foot, pinning it to the ground. He screamed and swung his arm, backhanding her into the wall. He raised his hand to hit her again but a furry bundle launched itself at him, followed immediately by Reg. He pinned Freddy to the ground.

Chatty's dog stood sentinel, growling.

Delia shook away the stars. J.B. and Geoffrey were no longer grappling on the ground. Panting for breath, they circled each other. Geoffrey managed to pull his gun without taking his eyes off J.B. His eyes were crazy and he didn't seem to notice the blood dripping out of his nose, oozing from his lip. J.B. swayed slightly. Delia picked up a rock and hurled at Geoffrey. She didn't hit him hard, but it was enough to throw off his aim. When the gun went off, the bullet went astray.

Geoffrey flung the gun at J.B. and rushed him. They grappled on the ground and Delia struggled to see who was gaining ground. Suddenly, J.B. reared up, raising his arms over his head. He held...his boot. He'd pulled off his boot and slammed it down on Geoffrey's head. One. Two. Three times.

And the fight was over.

Geoffrey groaned, but didn't try to stand up. Reg sat on Freddy. Delia struggled to her feet while J.B. put his boot back on. They rushed together, falling into each other's arms.

"Are you hurt?" J.B. asked, gently running his hand over the growing bruise on her cheek where Freddy had hit her.

"No, no, I'm fine. Are you hurt?" Delia rushed out. J.B. shook his head. He pulled her in tighter, and then pushed her away, a hand on each shoulder.

"Delia, we're getting married. Body or no body." He didn't look like he was willing to accept anything else, but that was fine with Delia. Her heart felt like it was going to burst. She reached out, putting her hands on either side of J.B.'s face. She slowly pulled him toward her. "Yes," she whispered.

Someone cleared his throat. It was Reg, looking embarrassed at seeing this personal moment. J.B. and Delia stepped away from each other, dropping their arms. After barely a pause, J.B. reached out and took Delia's hand, holding it in his. He stood by her side and Delia felt as if together, they could face any foe.

Reg had tied up Freddy and now stood over Uncle Geoffrey, still prone on the ground. "That's one heck of a boot you got there, J.B."

They all looked at the groaning man, holding a hand against the pain in his head. "I've got a wood block in that one boot. It's hollow. Or, it was. Now it's filled with gold. Heavy gold." J.B. smiled and squeezed Delia's hand.

Delia felt a tug on her skirt. It was Chatty's dog.

"We wouldn't have found you so soon if it wasn't for this dog's love of your soap," said J.B.

Delia slipped her hand from J.B.'s and knelt down. "It's time we give you a name," she said as she petted the dog. Suddenly, he looked to the entrance of the cave and growled. A moment later, they heard Michael Flaherty's voice call out.

"How are things, J.B.? I've got some fellows here ready to aid you."

J.B. looked into Delia's eyes as she stood again at his side. "Couldn't be better," he called out. He held her hand and they walked out of the cave together. "I've found the mother lode."

EPILOGUE

The door burst open and blast of cold air and bright light shot through the cabin. J.B. stumbled in, tripping over the dog at his feet.

"Dawsy! Get out of my way," he grumbled to the dog. They were both covered with a dusting of snow. Delia jumped up and quickly closed the door. She began brushing the snow off of J.B.'s coat and then took the basket from J.B.'s hands. She peered inside.

"Eggs! How did you get fresh eggs?" Her mouth watered at the thought.

"Reg made a trade with some fellow who has chickens laying inside his nice warm cabin." He shuffled over to the stove and held out his hands to warm them. He glanced around their cabin. "I'm not sure I'm willing to share the cabin with chickens. It's hard enough with a wife and dog."

Delia raised her eyebrows at him. J.B. grinned. She shook her head.

"Is Reg joining us for supper?" she asked, walking over beside J.B.

"Afraid not," said J.B. as he slipped his arm around Delia. They stood together in the circle of the stove's warmth. "He's going to a meeting about local law. He was real perturbed by the posse that ran off with Geoffrey and Freddy and hung them, without due process of law. He's finally got the Sheriff willing to listen to him, and that's today."

"Is he still mad at Michael?"

J.B. nodded. "Michael wasn't trying to create a posse. He was just bringing help to find you. But Reg thinks Michael didn't try hard enough to stop them." Delia waited, knowing what would come next. "I'm afraid I didn't try as hard as I could have. I was just glad to have you back and the trouble over."

Delia rested a hand on J.B.'s chest. "Let's think about something else, J.B." J.B. placed his hand over hers, sliding it until it rested over his heart. She waited until he nodded. "I have a project for you. Something to pass the time on these cold winter's days."

J.B. waggled his brow. Delia laughed and slapped him on the shoulder. "Not that!" She wondered if he could see her blush in the dim light. "A carving project." She tried to look serious but could feel the corners of her mouth turning up. "I'd like you to carve a cradle."

J.B. grabbed Delia up and swung her around, yelling "Wahoo!" The cabin shook and a dusting of snow snuck in through the shutters.

J.B. stopped spinning her and they stood together, grinning. He placed a hand on her stomach. "You're having a baby?"

"I am. We are," she said.

J.B.'s eyes met hers. "Better than gold," he said.

THANK YOU SO MUCH FOR READING! IF YOU ENJOYED THIS book, please take a moment to leave a review.

The next book in this series, about former lawman and now owner of the mercantile in Virginia City, Reg Smith, is called <u>Moving Mountains</u>.

Read on for a sneak peek.

SNEAK PEEK, MOVING MOUNTAINS

MARCH 1866, VIRGINIA CITY, MONTANA TERRITORY

The wagon couldn't proceed because of the mob in the street. Josie leaned out the side, her fellow passengers crowding around her. They'd just arrived in Virginia City and hadn't even reached the hotel yet. But the town, reported to have more than seventy saloons, was living up to its reputation as a wild mining town.

Two men squared off in the street. They circled each other, animal snarls on their faces. This was no professional boxing match with fighters dancing on their feet. They stumbled and tripped over the dirt around them, frozen in some spots and muddy in others. They were surrounded by cheering and jeering men.

The taller one lunged forward, his fist connecting with the jaw of the other. The shorter one fell to one knee, his hat falling off. Shouts and groans erupted. The taller one reached out his hand to catch a bottle tossed his way. He took a swig and threw the bottle back.

The shorter man revived from his stumble, wiping spittle from his lips. The two men continued to circle each other.

"Josie, move over!" Gladys elbowed her in the side.

"Gladys, you had your turn on the outside already!" Josie said.

"How was I supposed to know Virginia City would be so interesting?"

Josie didn't bother to answer. She strained to reach further out of the coach, pushing the canvas cover higher out of her way. The fighters were in the middle of the street that was stocked with numerous saloons, a billiard hall, a mercantile, a lawyer's office, and a butcher's shop. The crowd surrounding the men extended up onto the boardwalk lining the buildings. At this moment, Josie couldn't see a single woman outside of the ones in their own wagon.

The shorter man roared and ran, shouldering his weight right into his opponent's middle and knocking them both to the ground.

"What's happening?" Jane squealed.

Josie tried to look past the shifting backs of the audience, occasionally catching a glimpse of the men rolling around on the ground.

"They're wrestling. The tall one's on top. No! Now the short one's on top. Now…now I can't see a bit."

The crowd roared and the circle around the fighters widened. The men had broken apart and lurched to their feet. There was a long pause and suddenly all sound stopped.

"What—?" Josie cut off Gladys with a slash of her hand.

"Shhh!"

The mob began scrambling and men dashed behind wagons and barrels, or at least up onto the boardwalks so that they could still see well. As the crowd thinned, Josie saw why. The two brawlers had pulled out their guns. Each one had his right arm pinned to his side, bent at the elbow to aim his pistol at the other. What was left of the mob divided into two sides, many of them perched on the boardwalks ready to dash inside a building if the gunfight got out of hand.

From the shadow of the mercantile store porch, a single man came forward. The man, wearing a jacket and kerchief necktie, vaulted over a hitching rail and landed directly between the two men wielding guns. He held his hands out, one toward each man as though he could hold them—or their bullets—back through sheer force of will.

He had broad shoulders and salt-and-pepper hair that would have made Josie think he was older, except that she'd just seen him jump over the hitching rail and land as smooth as molasses. And he was handsome. Terribly handsome.

"What's he saying?" Mary asked, trying to brace herself on Josie so she could lean out further. Josie shoved her back in.

"I don't know!" She could hear the forceful tone of his deep voice but not the actual words. "They're walking toward him!"

Mary, peering over Josie's shoulder, said, "Listen to the crowd. They don't like him breaking up the fight."

"No," breathed Josie, "but they're accepting it. The fighters —they're putting their guns in their holsters. I think the fight is over—"

Before she could finish, the new man reached out, cupped each man around the back of the head and knocked their heads together. The crowd roared again. He then grabbed both men by the scruff of their necks. He spun them around and walked them eight paces to a horse trough and dunked them right in. He pulled them out and let them drop into the mud.

This time, Josie heard him. "The days of street shootouts are past. We've got doctors and families and a lending library even. Get out of here and sober up!"

He turned his back and walked to the boardwalk in front

of the store. Some men patted him on the back as he stepped up. Others scowled at him as they paid off their losing bets to some other smiling fellows. Then, suddenly, the man spun around. He looked over the heads of the men milling in the street, over the two brawlers stumbling away together, right at Josie.

He didn't smile or smirk. But he stared. And she stared back. They were connected like a telegraph wire without a message. But the message was coming. Josie could feel it.

The driver called out and the wagon lurched forward. Josie pulled herself back inside. Reluctantly.

To read the rest of the story, get your copy of <u>Moving Mountains</u>.

Dana Alden lives in Bozeman, Montana with her husband and children. Dana has lived in Canada, Japan, and parts of the U.S., but her heart is in Montana. Dana writes the Mountain Men of Montana Series and the Darlington Family Saga Series.

Stay in touch! If you'd like to know when Dana's next book releases, please visit her website at www.DanaAlden.com and join her mailing list.